HIS STEADFAST LOVE

AND OTHER STORIES

a collection by Paul Brownsey

His Steadfast Love and Other Stories
by Paul Brownsey
Copyright © 2015 Paul Brownsey
All Rights Reserved

ISBN 978-1-59021- 438-1 / 1-59021-438-2

Cover art by Elizabeth Leggett
Cover design by Inkspiral Design
Interior formatting by Kody Boye

Lethe Press, Inc.
118 Heritage Ave, Maple Shade, NJ 08052
lethepressbooks.com

To Jim,
with love.

TABLE OF CONTENTS

TRUE IN MY FASHION

I am very happy with Kenneth but the relationship involves a lie. I told it thirty-three years ago.

If you distinguish big lies from little lies, mine was only a little lie. It is not, for instance, that I have a wife and children but have lied to keep them from Kenneth's knowledge all these years.

Nor is my lie anything like that told me by someone I was with before Kenneth, a person who said he was a television producer for BBC Scotland. I thought that his run-down two-roomed flat in Partick was a bit of a dump for a top BBC producer, but he said that it was just a pied-à-terre and that his real home was a big house in Helensburgh where, unfortunately, we couldn't go because his mother lived there. One room had bare boards and an old vinyl settee and a television. The other contained a cooker and dripping sink, a wee Formica-topped table, three stacking chairs, a shower cabinet, and a mattress on the floor where we had sex.

Once, he told me that Debbie Harry was coming to dinner with us at the pied-à-terre. Then it was that she'd cancelled because of flying to New York to record a duet with Darryl Hall but had sent me a present as apology. I looked at the album, which was signed in her name with love to me, and thought how the bed sheets always reeked of cooking smells, which implied he stayed there a lot.

One night, Kenneth came up to me in the bar and told me that my BBC producer was just a clerk in Glasgow Council's cleansing department.

When I learned he was not what he'd said he was, I was not upset or angry with him. You need to know a person for that, and here I felt I did not know anyone, because he had deceived me about himself. If a tree in the park dematerialised before my eyes, I wouldn't feel shock or alarm, because it would be too weird and disorienting for ordinary feelings.

No, my lie was nothing gross like that.

My lie was to claim to have written a poem I hadn't. In fact, the poem was a song lyric by Irving Berlin.

Kenneth was chunky and open-faced and bright-eyed. He said "Great stuff" and "Okeydokey" a lot, and he soon adopted "No problem" when it came in. At first I treated all this as a front behind which there had to be weakness and self-doubt, but by the time he spilled the beans about my television producer/cleansing clerk I had never noticed a single chink in him through which that stuff could be glimpsed. It still amazes me that in those days Kenneth could be so ready to live together, buy a house together, and so on, without any fear of going public as a gay couple, exposed to neighbours and family and employers, whereas this fear pervaded most of us so completely we didn't realise it was there and thought we were caused to act only by passion or its absence.

He said he was telling me about the television producer/housing clerk because he wanted to protect me from hurt and then I heard coming from the dance floor Debbie Harry singing "Heart Of Glass". It was hard not to see this as a sign, a record by someone about whom I had been lied to playing just when I had been enlightened about the man who told the lie (and forged Debby Harry's signature and love on the album).

Actually, I knew there are no signs and everything is

just chance events.

I said to Kenneth, "May I have this dance with you?" Note the phrase.

Later that night, in bed, he said to me, "You were so formal," and he laughed. It was not the hurtful mocking laughter of someone who sits outside the world and finds you an object of amusement, but the upholding laughter that spills over from love.

He said, laughing further, "So formal that I was expecting you to say, 'May I perform fellatio upon you?' Then he hugged me like he was a wall against the world, and so we were happy together at once.

Be patient. I am getting to my lie.

I love musicals, though now I have to keep the fact from Kenneth. I once read that Irving Berlin wrote a huge number of songs in which some aspect of dancing features as a metaphor for some aspect of love: "Change Partners" and "Cheek To Cheek" and "Let's Face The Music And Dance" and "It Only Happens When I Dance With You", etc. One of his early efforts was "May I Have This Life With You?" This, obviously, is a play upon the traditional formal request for a dance—the formal request that Kenneth laughed at in such a wonderful way the night we became an item. Berlin wrote it to the tune that he later recycled as "The Hostess With The Mostest" in *Call Me Madam*. Berlin did that sort of thing. The song everyone knows as "Easter Parade" began life as "Smile And Show Your Dimple"

Well, because "May I Have This Life With You?" echoed what I said to Kenneth on our first night and also because the words expressed what I truly felt and still feel, I wrote the lyric in my first Valentine to him:

PAUL BROWNSEY

May I have this life with you-oo?
Let me take you by the hand.
It's a life just made for two-oo,
Dancing to a ragtime band.
And if we match steps to the rhythm this whole life through
We'll be in each other's arms for the next one too.

"Did you write this?" Of course he got the allusion to my invitation at once. He gave his laugh that honours a treasured possession.

"Yes."

I am not going to deny responsibility and say *I don't know what came over me* or *It was just a sudden mad impulse.* In olden days people might even have said *An evil spirit spoke through me.*

That would be denying I was a person, if lies just sort of popped out of me.

And it would be dishonest to pretend that my *Yes* referred just to the physical act of writing the lyric on the card.

After I said, "Yes," Kenneth kissed me and said, "Re your request re having this life with me, no problem at all."

I hear you saying, "Is that it? *That's* your lie? Come on! It was harmless enough."

Or: "Well, if you are so troubled by it decades later, just tell him."

No.

"Would he dump you for having lured him in by deceit and false pretences?"

Of course not. Our love has acquired its own weight and permanence totally independently of that lie.

"Well, there you are, then. Tell him, and he'll laugh— you go on about his laughter. You'll laugh *together*, the moment will enhance you both, and then you can move on."

I cannot tell him. I don't tell lies. That is who I am. I'm not like my BBC producer/cleansing clerk.

My lie has had consequences.

I was afraid that Kenneth might find me out in my lie. He delights so much to please me that it would have been like him to seek out for me discs of little-known musicals. I pictured something arriving from America with a title like *The Unknown Irving Berlin*. Removing it from its packaging prior to wrapping it in beautiful gift-wrap for my birthday or Christmas he glances at the list of the titles, and, since he can never forget the words of my first Valentine to him, it leaps out at him: "May I Have This Life With You?" Out of curiosity he plays it. He discovers I lied.

So I made a point of saying from time to time, "I don't know why, but I've gone off musicals, somehow." When he got us tickets for the 1987 London production of *Follies*, I gave a complicated performance in which I acted the delight I really felt but deliberately added apparently unintentional hints that I was only pretending to be pleased so as to not to hurt his feelings. ("I don't know why, but I've gone off musicals, somehow, but, of course, *this* is different.") The more successful I was in this the more I hurt his feelings, but needs must.

The consequences did not stop there. Although I *said*, "I don't know why, but I've gone off musicals, somehow," I hadn't, and when the CD era hit its stride and there was a vogue for reissuing old musicals on CD, I couldn't resist. Such treasures! Of course, things like the Original Broadway Cast album of *My Fair Lady* and the soundtracks of the main Rodgers and Hammerstein films would always be available, reissued again and again. But there was a lot of stuff that would only have a brief life in the catalogues, long-forgotten Broadway musicals like *Christine*, starring Maureen O'Hara, no less. So I bought them but hid them. I told Kenneth that one drawer contained all my childhood diaries and while, of course, he could read them if he wanted to—for there were no secrets between us—still, I said, I had a sort of irrational squeamishness about anyone reading them. Which of course produced a promise he wouldn't look at them.

"Anyway," he said, "They wouldn't show me the you that I love. Love this whole life through, remember."

You may be thinking that this is a moralistic lesson about how one lie leads to more lies, a web of lies, like for want of a nail the kingdom was lost.

No, that's not the point at all.

"But when," you say, "did you listen to these CDs? Surely it was no different from not having them at all, not being able to play them?"

Oh, but possession is a bulwark.

And something might happen that would allow me to play them freely, for instance, Kenneth's death.

Of course, they might undergo that process of CD decay called bronzing and become unplayable, but to be on the safe side I stored second copies of particular favourites, preferably different pressings so that if one bronzed the other might not. I have also started secretly putting them on an mp3 player, but Kenneth isn't often away so I don't get much opportunity for that.

Sometimes I take a horrifying risk. I put a musicals CD in a classical music case and in Kenneth's presence put on the CD and listen to it through headphones. Suppose Kenneth suddenly notices the CD case while I am listening to, say, *Kiss Me, Kate*, and says, "Hey, Beethoven's Fifth, fantastico," and presses the button to channel the sound through the loudspeakers? That would crack open all the defences that the world has put in place.

There's safer listening to my musicals CDs when Kenneth's Dad comes on the 'phone saying he's scared he might have a stroke and lie there unfound. Then Kenneth goes and spends a night or two at his sheltered housing— he won't come here because he's homophobic—and while Kenneth sleeps badly on the settee and cleans the house and helps the old man shuffle to and from the bathroom, I enjoy the guilty pleasure of *Belle*, a 1961 British musical about Dr Crippen that flopped in the West End, or *Skyscraper*, a dull and awkward Broadway musical from 1965 starring Julie Harris that's redeemed by one song, the sublime, "I'll Only Miss Her When I Think Of Her," which, when I play it, in my mind changing the sex like in the Peggy Lee recording, is about me thinking of Kenneth at his Dad's.

Sometimes on these evenings alone I think it would be only poetic justice if it were I, not Kenneth's Dad, who had the stroke and died alone. Kenneth would find me stretched out cold, the musicals CDs lying around the living-room to prove my untruthfulness while, blasting out again and again on repeat, Mitzi Gaynor sang about being, like I am, in love with a wonderful guy.

But if this poetic justice occurred, it would have this comfort: there is a pattern, the universe is being administered, things happen because they are meant to, the risk is not from chance events.

Of course, someday I shall indeed die, and Kenneth, sorting my things, will unlock the drawer. If he was telling the truth when he said he didn't want to read my diaries, he won't discover it's locked till then. He'll then discover I lied about it containing diaries and lied about having gone off musicals, but discovering these lies won't reveal my lie about the poem. Still, it will be like the stashes of pornography that wives sometimes find and write to agony aunts about: "To think that when we make love he is fantasising about…suddenly a stranger to me…never known him at all." And he won't be able to tell himself they're just a hangover from the days when I liked musicals, because a lot of them have recent issue-dates on them. I don't like to leave Kenneth with all that distress, but there is something in me, some little core of self-destruction or self-preservation, that prevents my getting rid of my musicals CDs, and I wouldn't do it even if managed to put them all on my mp3 player.

But I am not without a way forward.

I have evidence that would allow me to believe that Kenneth has forgotten that I wrote what I did in that card. In itself that is sad, but the good outweighs the evil. Safety is part of the quality of life, not a substitute for it.

There is a programme about musicals on the radio on Sunday afternoons, usually hosted by Elaine Paige.

One Sunday the programme came on unexpectedly while I was making dumplings in the kitchen, dough all over my fingers. It would have been too significant, too likely to arouse suspicion of a weakness in my defences, to go across and turn it off with mucky fingers. Kenneth was cleaning his shoes and mine at the back door behind me.

Elaine started talking about composers recycling things. Richard Rodgers recycled "Beneath The Southern Cross" from *Victory At Sea* as "No Other Love" in *Me And Juliet*. "Getting To Know You" in *The King And I* began life as "Suddenly Lovely" for *South Pacific*.

Furiously, I scraped surplus dough off my fingers with

the kitchen knife.

"Say A Prayer For Me Tonight", cut from *My Fair Lady*, ended up in *Gigi*. "And," says Elaine, "Irving Berlin's 'Hostess With The Mostest'—"

The scraped-off dough was bloody, a little flap of skin hung from a finger.

"—started life like *this!*"

> *May I have this life with you-oo?*
> *Let me take you by the hand…*

The gushing of the cold water tap on my finger wasn't enough to drown the ancient crackly male voice.

Shouting and hollering about my wound would create a diversion but something thrawn stopped me.

> *…It's a life just made for two-oo…*

Now Kenneth was actually singing along, shoe-brushing to the rhythm.

And then Ethel Merman's abrasive voice poured out relief upon me as the engineers did a clever thing, seamlessly merging "May I Have This Life With You?" into "The Hostess With The Mostest." A comet out of nowhere had missed the earth by a hairsbreadth and was now on its way back to outer space.

I mean, he knew the words but he didn't say he'd recognised them as what I'd written in my card, did he? So I don't have to think he did.

"You know," Kenneth said, gathering up the shoe-cleaning stuff, "I don't know why, but I could quite get to like musicals, somehow. Christ, what have you done?"

I don't know why, but I've gone off musicals, somehow. Yes, what he said echoed what I'd said, but so what?—It's well known that couples unconsciously influence each other.

"Give me your hand," he said. "Let me take you by the hand."

"May I perform first-aid upon you?" he said, dabbing and pressing my bloody finger with sheets of kitchen towel until the blood stopped flowing. He fetched and attached a plaster. It was grubbied by a fingerprint of shoe-polish because he'd been too caught up in alarm about me to wash his hands first.

"All mended," he said.

"Well…"

"No problemo. No problem at all."

So the chance event of this radio programme has opened the way to a scenario which saves the situation. I can choose in all honesty to believe that Kenneth has forgotten I quoted the lyric in my card; meanwhile, he gets to really like musicals, which allows me to discover that actually I like them after all ("I don't know why, but I've gone onto musicals again, somehow"), which means we start buying lots of musicals CDs ("It's much nicer to have the physical object than just to download them"), which allows me gradually to slip in among the ones on our open shelves the ones from the locked drawer, which means I prevent the shameful revelation after I am dead that I lied about going off musicals, which lie was to prevent him discovering the lie about the lyric I told thirty-three years ago. The world survives, renews itself, and Kenneth's love continues to protect me from bad things breaking in, although, of course, because of his love nothing was ever really at risk anyway.

ANOTHER PERSON'S BONES

They have hoisted a wall-unit together and have just begun their interdependent shuffle with it to the kitchen wall. Footsteps crunch on the gravel outside, a voice commands: "We're here." Only then comes the rat-a-tat at the front door.

David whispers, "Bugger, they're early. But we can still hide. Just keep still. They can't see us through the window."

Footsteps crunch again, moving round the building. "Pretty derelict. Whatever could have got into him?" The voice is unafraid of being overheard.

"It's the sort of project many people like, renovating an old village school." Marion's judicious voice. In the course of her marriage to Lennox she has constituted herself a judicious person who has projects.

David cannot see Stephen's face, only his forearms either side of the wall-unit, which is in an inappropriate style chosen by Stephen called Siciliano. The shirtsleeves have been meticulously rolled back, because that is what you do when you get down to physical labour. David passes the time trying hard to see those forearms as those of a stranger. They are white, plumpish, almost hairless.

The forearms tremble.

"You losing hold?" Whispered.

"No." Whispered back from the other side of Siciliano. David hears the throaty catch, almost gurgle, that means that what is coming is one of Stephen's very conscientious attempts to apply official procedures for being humorous, lightsome. "We are like settlers in a log cabin hiding from Red Indians."

So it's silent laughter that's making the forearms tremble. No, coming from Stephen it's a sort of *performance* of laughter: Stephen knows that laughter is a thing people do, sometimes.

Whatever it is David has gained, he feels the loss of his whole soul. Once again he'll need to rev up within himself the David who's got life under control. He's enviable, that David: he's ageless (the fairish hair standing up like a brush helps here), he's at home anywhere (he has this careless ability to wear blue denims with a smart navy jacket without any incongruity at all), he's always got the answer.

"A face-up there!" Stephen has been surprised into speaking out loud.

They were seen. David roars too heartily, "Coming, coming." The aquiline face of the Reverend Lennox Burnett had ascended briefly into view in the fanlight above the kitchen door, followed by a jump-concluding gravelly crunch. Having position and Christian charity, Lennox has never seen a need for dignity.

Siciliano is set down, the door opened. "Sorry. You caught us in the middle of shifting something."

Lennox stares disapprovingly into the gutted kitchen, Marion appraisingly. Lennox rebukes: "You got my card saying we'd call."

"No." Later David will realise that the ease with which he shows pleasure at the unexpected arrival of his oldest friend owes something to glimpsing Stephen laying the do-it-yourself manual on top of Lennox's postcard on the kitchen table .

While Marion looks for a task for her to perform and

finds it in holding out her hand to Stephen, saying, "I've been so looking forward to meeting you," Lennox sidles past abandoned Siciliano into the sitting-room. He glances out at the Aberdeenshire countryside beyond the playground wall. It rears up, rolls away in pale February sunshine.

"Well, you've got the view." Contemptuously. "But where are your customers to come from, David? Not a house in sight."

Stephen takes the chance to make a contribution. "There are quite a lot of farms and crofts, and we're between two quite large villages, and neither of them has a shop. And it's not as if—"

"And what will you do for company, David? Is there a soul within twenty miles you can exchange two intelligent words with?"

David has wondered that, too.

He speaks with easy confidence. "As Stephen was about to say"—pause to point up Lennox's rudeness—"it's not as if I'm out to make a fortune. As if we are. So long as the shop just ticks over. And if the worst comes to the worst, Stephen can always go back to being a lawyer. Aberdeen's not that far." When he hears Lennox say, "So *you'll* be kept. Well, well," he hurries on: "As for company, our nearest neighbour is Annie, in a cottage about a quarter of a mile away. She's eighty-two. Came here from Harris to be near her son, Murdo Angus, who married a local girl and works in the grounds of our local country house hotel. We go to Annie for ceilidh - it just means socialising, you know - at least twice a week and hear about the latest delays over her hip-replacement operation."

As expected, Lennox rises to the challenge to be appalled, for he has no doubt that everyone is equal in

God's eyes.

"Solitary confinement in the back of beyond! You'll go mad within three months, begging the BBC to have you back."

"Oh, but that's the view of someone from a city, where other people are just an entertainment and there are always new faces to distract you from old ones. Where people are disposable. Here in the country people are few and precious and you appreciate each person in their fulness, there's a sort of rootedness in each other, it's a different way of being. It's *real* human connection." David hears in his voice how far he is from being the person who believes this; though, true, he did put a bit of deflecting irony into it.

"Theology." Contemptuously. "That may have been all right when we were students, David. Do we get the guided tour?"

As they go through the door that connects the school house with the single large classroom, still stacked with boxes and furniture from their separate flats in Glasgow, Stephen takes it on himself to say, "We can't make any structural changes. That was a condition." Here it comes, the sawing gurgle, the machinery of conversational wit clanking up. Has no-one ever mentioned it to him, like a close friend dropping you a hint about bad breath?

Stephen says, "We shall probably find ourselves writing up our special offers for dog food and oven chips and toilet rolls on the old school blackboard." Which is, of course, not there.

Lennox confides his musing to the world at large: "People in rural Aberdeenshire may not wish to purchase from a shop run by *two men*." But Marion smiles appreciatively at Stephen and says, "What I'd like would be if you found piles of old exercise books." She says it with such authority that David and Lennox are transformed into by-standers. Marion's face is broad and bony like her body. She has dark circles round her eyes which make her look guilt-ridden. David remembers her saying, a year after she married Lennox, "I think I need to find something to take an interest in," and at that time the history of rural education in Scotland had seemed a more or less random choice of project, nothing to be said for or against. Now she is an acknowledged expert on it, she sits on committees, she has a book coming out, her enthusiasm is infectious as she continues, "I have a theory that rural literacy a century ago, even with children of all ages being taught in the same room sometimes, was far higher than among children today. I've seen letters written by a village girl in Towie to her brother in the trenches that are astonishingly capable in their use of language."

They all make remarks about literacy for a while, so that it does not seem at all a contrivance when Marion declines to go outside, saying, "Oh, I'll stay here and talk to Stephen."

In the weedy hard-trodden playground Lennox leads the way towards a brick outbuilding with "Boys" and "Girls" picked out in the concrete lintels. "All right, I suppose."

"Yes, the place needs a lot doing to it, but—"

"Him!"

Lennox halts long enough for his eyes to emphasise David's misconstrual. It always seems a shame to David that the Church of Scotland can't offer Lennox the rank and office of prince-bishop. "What is he, thirty-five, forty? Still got his blond boyish good looks but they're getting a bit chubby. He'll suddenly put on a lot of weight and go slack. Not much intelligence or taste. Do for a bit, I suppose. An improvement on Billy Gotta, anyway. Ah, David."

The last two words offer a homecoming as, behind the children's lavatories, Lennox opens his arms. When David does not move Lennox steps forward, embraces him, runs his hands up and down David's body, grunts with satisfaction.

A little while after Lennox's hands have come to rest on David's buttocks, David steps out of the embrace.

"Whatever's worrying you? They can't see us here."

David says quickly, "Haven't thought of Billy Gotta for ages."

"*Haven't* you." Not a question.

"Poor little Billy. 'I gotta be true to my love, whatever it costs me.' 'I know I gotta think of his pleasure as well as my own.' He actually said that out loud, in bed."

Lennox contributes: "I gotta see this through by myself." He makes no attempt at an American accent on "gotta".

Awkward moment passed, harmless reminiscences flowing. David pulls up some tall weeds. "'I gotta remember that you gotta pay your dues for the love you get.' 'I gotta get through to my family that I gotta live my own life.' I suppose he got 'I gotta' from some American film. 'Gahdah.' The Glaswegian need for Americanisms. Even about his overdose. Took the pills, then had a shower, then stood there absolutely naked dripping all over the carpets in the lamplight: 'I gotta get to a doctor, I swallowed all the aspirins in the bathroom.'"

"I don't suppose you'll have that sort of problem with this latest one. Lawyers don't say 'I gotta'. And you're okay for our annual Glyndebourne jaunt? Te Kanawa as the

Countess."

"Stephen doesn't like opera."

Finding images for his situation sometimes helps David feel reconciled to it. The image that comes to him most often is that in Stephen he glimpsed a golden god, and now the god has departed, leaving behind disconnected things like, oh, that scraping gurgle in the throat, and those weirdly waxy forearms, and the particular pause and faint frown when David wants to make love (no automatically answering desire) and then the absolutely meticulous performance. Scattered phenomena like these, with no-one inside them, let alone a god, are what you have to make yourself fit to live with.

Now a different image stirs. Just formulating it will have some power to comfort but Lennox's reply interrupts: "Just as well. I've only got the two tickets as usual. Could be awkward having him along. Looks the sulky possessive type. Would get po-faced about you and me having our little half hours to ourselves."

A high horse is conveniently at hand. "Lennox, can't you see it'll need to finish, you and me sloping off every so often? What Marion must have felt all these years!" He makes an effort to feel it for her.

"Marion has her interests, too."

"Oh yes, she trawls the archives, you troll for men. And old David once in a while."

"Chubby-chops is making you priggish."

David peeps round the edge of the lavatory block as though to ensure none of this can be heard back in the main building. One more sacrifice to a god who doesn't exist: "I won't be coming to Glyndebourne, Lennox." The sky is resolutely sunless now, the afternoon cold.

"Well, if you're *that* frightened he'll run off while you're away…"

"It's not like that. We've bought this place jointly. It's his as much as mine. A project that will bring us together."

"'Will bring us together.'" Lennox's voice underscores the future tense. He nods several times at his penetration of how things stand in the present. "Love in a cottage, that's what they used to call it in the eighteenth century, this romantic whim for a cosy poor-but-happy rural idyll. You'll soon be looking for love in another sort of cottage." He smirks at his ease with the slang for a public lavatory. "You're not the sort of person who can be *brought together* with anyone for long. Billy Gotta!"

David pleads: "But you can become the sort, can't you? The sort who will settle for…. Who will settle." The high horse neighs. "I wouldn't have thought a minister of the Kirk would have any trouble with the idea of trying to make yourself into a particular sort of person. Trying to put into place within yourself another person's bones. The bones of the person you're committed to becoming. Isn't it called being born again?"

"Theology again." Incredulity: "You actually believe you can do it."

"Lord, I believe. Help thou my unbelief."

Abruptly Lennox leaves the shelter of the lavatory block. Dusk is falling. As David follows him back to the main building Lennox says, "This Annie. You must give me details. I knew one of the geriatrics people up here when he was in Edinburgh. Maybe speed things up."

Indoors they all take tea. They talk about the various repairs and improvements that David and Stephen are making, and it is as part of the general conversation that Lennox asks for the lavatory. David indicates the stairs, which ascend from an alcove off the sitting-room. "Top of the stairs, first on the right." They listen to him ascending the stairs. A little later they hear the flush.

Stephen is saying to Marion: "Coming back to what we were talking about"—what *did* they talk about while David and Lennox were outside? —"I wouldn't want to think too much about my neighbours' levels of literacy. It would be to judge them and distance myself from them. You have to set that sort of thing aside for a real human connection." Once again David winces mentally at his life-sentence.

There is still no sound of Lennox descending.

Stephen cannot possibly mean what he's just said, it's not his sort of remark at all, it's just a mindless echo of David's flight about relating to people in the country. Except that where David poised teasingly between pretentiousness and irony Stephen attempts earnestness.

David cuts him down: "One can't help judging people. It's part of being conscious of them."

The crash and the indignant yell happen together, confusion and dust and bits descend, Lennox's foot and ankle have appeared through the sitting-room ceiling. The sock is patterned in black and white diamonds. The foot wriggles; lumps of plaster, more clouds of dust, are dislodged. His cries contain no panic, address underlings: "Help. Help."

David rushes for the stairs. Opposite the lavatory, to the left as you come up the stairs, is an odd little room that he and Stephen have talked of fitting up to hang clothes in. Their bedroom opens off it. The bedroom door opens inwards and the light switch is awkwardly placed behind the hinge of the door. When David flicks it on Lennox is revealed trapped between the joists of the floor. His free leg writhes a little as though of its own accord. The double bed sits on an island of floorboards towards the far wall.

"I don't think I mentioned that a lot of the floorboards in our bedroom are being replaced."

Lennox speaks towards the bed. "Billy Gotta is dead."

As David, balancing on joists and stooping, places his hands experimentally under Lennox's arms, Lennox adds, "Since you were talking of disposable people."

"If I haul, can you pull yourself up? How on earth do you know?"

"You're hauling too delicately. Use some effort. I took the funeral two weeks ago. AIDS."

Lennox wriggles and scrabbles, gradually he is extracted from the ceiling below, is helped to crawl across the joists to the ante-room. "But why you to conduct it?" Lennox can't stand on the leg that went through. If it's something permanently crippling, like an irreparable tendon—well, presumably you grow into being a person who is permanently crippled.

With help he can hobble. He says, "I don't think *I* mentioned something, either. Never lost touch with him. Not since the night you told him you didn't want him any more, and he took an overdose. And then a shower. And you were too drunk to drive him to the hospital and 'phoned me to do it. Dressed by that time so I didn't have the benefit of.... Hair still wet from his shower, though. Baptism into a new life when you've been cast aside and taken a fatal number of aspirins? Theology again. Got him somewhere to stay since you didn't want him back in your flat. And a job. Turned up on our doorstep from time to time over the years. Glad to see him. Sweet. Marion liked him, too. Not that I ever laid a finger on him. Or anything else. Toothsome, though. That wiry body, that anxious working-class look of expecting to come off worst. Trying so hard. 'I guess I gotta try and profit from the experience.""

"Lennox, it was twenty-odd years ago. I was, what, twenty-six. I was desperate to be in love, I'd dreamed so much of living happily ever after with someone. Okay, I chose someone totally unsuitable. I was inexperienced. Or put it down to wild oats. Whatever. It wasn't going to work out, that was clear."

"Clear after all of two weeks."

"I just didn't realise it could drive you mad, the sudden total proximity that makes you feel you've thrown your life away."

He adds, "Christ, he didn't really mean it. If you really mean to kill yourself, you don't then take a shower and run out and say you've got to get to a doctor. Manipulating wee toe-rag and bad at it." He says it affectionately, though.

For some time they've been positioning to descend the stairs. Lennox says, "Perhaps you're thinking, 'He was a loving, loyal boy. If I'd not booted him out, if I'd settled down with him, he'd probably be alive today.' But you mustn't torment yourself, David. *Not* your responsibility. At all."

Stephen is waiting at the foot of the stairs and they are only half-way down when he blazes at Lennox: "What the hell were you doing in our bedroom?"

Lennox will not tell a lie, so it's necessary for David to drag his eyes from Stephen towards Marion, urgently cueing her to say something in accordance with her lifelong project of making the way of Lennox straight.

Stephen's anger: nothing like the performance of indignation David supposes he has to attempt in court ("My Lord, there is not a *shred* of evidence..."). David realises he will always be the person who was astonished by that anger.

Marion continues to stare out the uncurtained window at the gathered darkness. David covers for her: "Sorry, Lennox, I should have warned you, this place is a warren of odd nooks and rooms off rooms, it's easy to lose your way."

"It's not easy at all. To get here from the loo you just come straight back down the stairs." Stephen, unassuaged.

Lennox has sat down. As if to distract them from distress at his injury, he says, "What perfect darkness. Not a light to be seen anywhere."

David tries to offer a flight: "Oh, but the one thing we don't want, Lennox, is lights shining in the distance, enticing us with glimmers of unknown delights, leading us on, luring us away from..." He sounds unbelieving and deflates into silence.

Stephen completes: "...from each other." The darkness outside gives the light in the sitting-room, and blond Stephen within it, a golden hue. He volunteers that they won't hear a word about paying for the damage to the ceiling: they've got to get the plasterer in for lots of other things anyway.

"I suppose I'd better get Lennox to casualty," says Marion, though she doesn't move. David, of course, takes an arm, puts it round his own shoulders. Lennox flaps the other, summoning another underling. Stephen inserts his shoulders beneath it. Lowering himself into the front passenger seat, Lennox slides his hand slowly down the length of Stephen's body just like someone giving himself support. When David goes to shut him in he says, "Less chubby than he looks. Do for a bit."

David shuts the door on him. Marion says, "Now. I think you two should come and see us quite often. Will you promise to?" The committee is being presented with the project it was too dunderheaded to devise for itself.

"It's okay, Lennox and I never really fall out."

"This has nothing to do with Lennox. Will you promise?" In that very building, no doubt, children were coaxed into promising teacher things for their own good.

They both say, "We promise," smiling a little. But Marion has another sanction, for then she speaks to Stephen at some length about how they'll have to be in touch quite a lot once he's had time to look up various things about the law relating to educational charities, which it seems he's going to advise her on.

Side by side they wave the Burnetts' car away. Stephen's hand is raised just as high as his own.

There it is, the gurgling little rasp. Think of being someone who finds it touching, lovable - no, who doesn't notice it at all. "Well, the brave settlers saw off the marauding Indians."

As they turn to go in - Stephen appears to have positioned himself for an arm to go round him, but, no, that's utterly unStephenlike, doesn't fit at all - the elusive image that had beckoned in the playground suddenly comes to David. It's as though he's a member of that tribe in New Guinea where you're condemned to carry strapped to your back forever the bones of someone who's died. Absurdly, he wants to tell Stephen this image he has of him, even opens his mouth to do so. It will, of course, be years and years before he can tell him.

TEA AT BALMORAL

Dennis saw her first, naturally enough since he was striding ahead up the glen in his beauties-of-nature-are-here-to-be-made-the-most-of way. I sulked along behind in the trainers I had worn in deliberate contrast to his regulation-issue walking boots.

"Your Majesty!" he cried, halting dramatically in a pose that expressed reverent alarm and distress.

Then he rushed towards her in an every-second-counts way but skidded to a halt about ten feet short. From that distance his stretching out first one arm and then the other was not a lot of use.

While Dennis flapped and fluttered I had extended a hand and she had grasped it. The ground treacherously concealed a burn, its bed a yard or so below the surface, its banks grown together leaving no detectable fissure in the ground. In good-quality green trousers, the Queen's left leg had disappeared into the hidden aperture, while her right leg was splayed out at ground level at an ominous angle.

She tried to raise herself; her face creased.

"You're in pain?"

Dennis's shocked look intimated that I ought to have been more circumspect about noticing pain in my sovereign.

"Both legs, actually. Rather severe. The knee in the one down there, and it's sort of in the groin in the other one." Dennis's eyes widened at the dangerous allusion.

"Dennis, if you took the Queen's hand on the other side it might actually help."

"Of course, Your Majesty." He wiped a hand on his calf-length hill breeches - Dennis believes in the proper clothing for everything - before extending it towards her, and only the firmness of her grip prevented him withdrawing it at her red-hot touch. In exasperation I reached my spare arm around the Queen's body and under the other arm. I detected no perfume, but that may have been because her thrashings sent up a rotten earthy smell from the peat.

I hauled, perhaps even Dennis hauled, and at last she was out of the fissure. The Queen lay before us on the grass. She looked very small. We were alone in the vast green landscape.

"Thank you." Perfect manners, of course.

"Thank *you*, Your Majesty."

I said, "Think you can stand?"

We each gave an arm.

"Dennis, hold your arm rigid. Give her some resistance to pull herself up on."

"I'm afraid it's my fault," said the Queen. "I don't seem to be able to put any weight on either leg."

So we just helped her to wriggle on her bottom out of the squelch and on to a tuft of grass, and then the question arose of what to do next.

"Robin can go for help, Your Majesty. I'd better stay here to make sure Your Majesty is, you know, all right."

"That's very kind," said the Queen, and Dennis smiled in his seraphic haven't-got-my-teeth-in way, though in fact he has all his own teeth.

I hurried back down the glen to the Visitor Centre at Spittal of Glenmuick, and because of what the Queen had told me to say I had no trouble in getting my story taken seriously. The man in charge immediately slammed a drawer shut, signalling that he, for one, knew his duty in the emergency that had come upon the world, and announced that the building was closed to the public. I asked if I should stay to direct the rescue party, but I was too irrelevant to receive a reply let alone escape being herded out the door along with two ladies in anoraks and a foreign-looking youth.

When I got back the Queen was still on her tuffet and Dennis was kneeling comfortably before her even though the knees of his breeches were soaking up the squelch. He had opened the packet of Mr Kipling Deep Filled Bramley Apple Pies we had brought to eat on our hike. The Queen held one and Dennis was encouraging her to eat it by eating another in a yum-yum-this-is-scrumptious way.

"Ah, here he is, Your Majesty. Help on the way? Well done that man! Your Majesty, I'd like to present my partner, Robin Murray."

From where Dennis stood her smile at me must have seemed all graciousness, but an almost undetectable amused lift of an eyebrow said to me, "Is he always like this?"

Dennis had on his twinkly-eyed-schoolmaster-not-really-angry-at-the-lads'-pranks look and was saying "Oh, he's got his faults, Your Majesty, like we all have—"

His worried look came over him, no doubt at the treasonable import of that "we all".

"Well, most of us, but I do hope you'll see, Your Majesty, that we're no different from anyone else, even though we are a gay couple. We're ready to lend a hand to someone in trouble, just like the Good Samaritan."

"Well, *of course.*" The Queen was very earnest, and from

the surprised delight on his face you'd have thought Dennis had never been quite sure of the point before.

I said, "Though I don't suppose that the original Good Samaritan, having paid the innkeeper to take care of the man who fell among thieves, then went off and had anonymous sex with a stranger in a public toilet. Did they have public toilets in first-century Israel?"

Dennis's glare strained to eliminate me, or at least what I had said, and the Queen said, "I don't know."

After a downcast pause Dennis regrouped. "What Robin meant to point out, Your Majesty, is that, it has to be admitted, there *is* a tiny minority of gay people who let the side down by conducting themselves in public places in ways which…" Something ebbed from him and his face showed just how much I'd wounded him. I felt awful. He gave up and concluded, "I'm very sorry, Your Majesty."

"So am I," I said.

Dennis perked up at once. "People look on us as outsiders, Your Majesty, as though we're, you know, aliens from Mars, not part of the community, but that's just not *true.*" His intensity of feeling was making wisps of hair stand out from his head.

"*Of course* it isn't true." Plea granted.

"I mean, Your Majesty, I, we, are just as patriotic as the next person. Just a small example, Your Majesty, I read in the 'paper that increasingly around the world orchestras and conductors are playing British composers. I really do feel a personal satisfaction in that. I *do*, and I'm not a great one for classical concerts. The Vienna Philharmonic are now playing Vaughan Williams!"

"Really?" Royal delight at the defeat of the Armada.

"And Sir Andrew, no, Lord Lloyd Webber, absolutely dominating Broadway, Your Majesty, Britain conquering the place where musicals came from. I mean, *I'm* sort of enlarged by that, I honestly am. That's how much I identify with Britain, even though I do happen to be gay. And Shakespeare, Dickens, Milton, Wordsworth - ah, we've got some world-beaters in literature! And Torville and Dean, no foreigner could touch them. There's something about seeing it in print, in the newspaper, 'Triumph for Britain'! And great events, state events, like Your Majesty's coronation, well, no-one else does them like us, do they?"

"No, I don't think they do," said the Queen, but in his haste to make it clear that he was not so impertinent as to demand a reply from his sovereign, he hurried on and talked over her: "And it all means just as much to me, to us, as it does to—"

"A normal person," I interjected helpfully.

Dennis was too smitten with earnestness to notice the momentary brightening of the Queen's eyes by which she told me she appreciated my little irony. She turned to him: "Oh dear, your knees are getting wet."

"So they are, Your Majesty." He laughed jovially and stayed put. "And Scotland, too. I mean, Your Majesty, it makes me feel grateful, that's the only word that will do, *grateful*, to have the privilege of belonging to a country that must have contributed more to the world than any other; you know, relative to population. I mean, logarithms, and Adam Smith, and television, and tarmac and anaesthetics and the telephone, Alexander Graham Bell, and…Your Majesty, Robin and I *always* spend our holidays here in our native Scotland." He paused imploringly like someone supplicating a touch for the King's Evil.

She was obliging enough to smile all the approval he wanted.

I said, "Anything to keep me off the nude beaches of Mykonos," and Dennis hurried on, "Oh, and I would just like to say that you, that Your Majesty, can rely on us absolutely as regards the Press. It's terrible, the hard time the Press give the royal family these days. I give you my word, Your Majesty, we won't breathe a word to the media about this. Or to anyone else. You can trust our word, Your Majesty. We may be gay, but our honesty and integrity are just as real as anyone else's."

"I am sure they *are* real."

"Your Majesty's trust makes *me* feel real." Coyly, but not unconscious that it was a courtier's tribute to rank with those of the Elizabethan wits and poets.

And then, bless him, out of the crassness came forth - well, whatever it was the prophet had who rebuked King David for his caryings-on over Bathsheba. Nathan's language was a probably a bit more impressive even before the author of 2 Samuel tarted it up.

"And it's because our integrity and honesty *are* real, Your Majesty, that I'm sorry to have to say, Your Majesty, that it's, well, not very nice, it's actually a sort of insult, what Your Majesty does at Buckingham Palace, not allowing gay people to bring their partners to the staff Christmas Ball."

He had risen to his feet like someone drawing himself up to his full height out of righteous anger, but now alarm shot across his face - perhaps it's contrary to court etiquette for a subject's head to be higher than the sovereign's - and at once he was back on his knees.

"I'm most grateful to you." A polite snub, a rote phrase to keep the impertinent at a distance and brush off the hungerers after royal intimacy.

No matter that after a moment's thought Dennis was

smiling seraphically again: I felt the avenging angel stir loyally on his behalf. I told the Queen very sincerely, "And if you feel it might help to talk over any members of your family, you know, Andrew or Edward, with people who know the score, well, feel free to 'phone up *any time.*"

You could hear the slow trickle of the hidden burn.

The Queen said, "Ah, here's help," and now she carefully laid down her unattempted apple pie on a rock. Around the bend in the track came in procession - but how else could they have come? - a jeep and three black estate cars. They seemed full of people, some in police uniform.

In no time a stretcher was unfolded from the jeep and two refined-looking men in Barbour jackets helped the Queen onto it. The others, nine or ten including two uniformed policewomen, had positioned themselves between us and her as though we might have chosen this moment to shoot her or stab her or bash her head in with a handy rock. No-one said anything to us.

The Queen made her bearers halt so that she could call, "Thank you so much, Mr Highet, Mr Murray." Remembering names is part of the job, of course.

Dennis had remained on his knees, absorbed in writing on what looked like a torn-off part of the apple pie box. Suddenly he stood up and plunged through the cordon in a they're-not-meant-to-keep-*me*-out way.

"I've written our names and addresses on this, Your Majesty. Our B and B address in Ballater as well as our permanent one in Glasgow. Just in case there's any need to, you know, contact us. About anything at all." He presented his piece of cardboard to the reclining Queen, who accepted it graciously.

"Thank you so much."

The vehicles moved off and, yes, the Queen smiled at us through glass and there was a wave a little more personal than the usual regal one.

Dennis said, "I bet we'll be hearing."

I encouraged him: "Sir Walter Raleigh got a knighthood for less."

"Oh, nothing so grand as that." Scornfully. "Perhaps an invitation to Balmoral, to tea, to sort of thank us properly. We'll need to tell Mrs Fordyce that we won't want a meal that night. I'll say we won't expect a reduction in the bill. It'll be worth it."

And all next day he refused to leave Mrs Fordyce's in case there was a summons from Balmoral. We were a bit under her feet in her cottage but she couldn't really complain because, as Dennis made a point of reminding her, she had the lounge-open-to-residents-all-day symbol in the tourist board brochure we'd got her address from. She made the best of it, bringing us tea and home-made cakes from time to time while we watched daytime television. "I think I overdid it a bit yesterday on our hike," he explained to her.

"She said she was most grateful to me," he said to me, meaning the Queen. "Well, I can believe she was. I bet we really opened her eyes, made her see gay people in a different light, and she's the sort of person to be grateful for that."

On the second day he did agree to go out, but telephoned Mrs Fordyce two or three times to ask if "an important 'phone call" he was expecting had come. True to his word to the Queen, he did not enlarge on the nature of the important 'phone call, but he emphasised rather too much that he couldn't say whom it might be from.

There was no call, and despite the speed with which he

drove us home at the end of our holiday, no letter from Balmoral awaited us, and none ever came.

Then we noticed the following paragraph in *Scotland on Sunday*:

QUEEN'S "SLIGHT" INJURY

The Queen wore a support bandage around her left leg when she made her traditional appearance at the annual Braemar Highland Gathering yesterday. A spokesman at Balmoral Castle, the royal family's holiday retreat on Deeside, said she suffered a slight sprain while walking on moorland on the estate. She was able to return to the castle without assistance and her doctor confirmed that the injury was not serious.

I said, "Grave cover-up of the truth. Shall I 'phone the 'paper or will you?"

"That would be breaking our word!" The shock in his voice was expected, for it was, after all, a proposal to contravene conventional morality, but I hadn't realised he'd been waiting for a springboard for one of his rare lettings-loose into real anger. "But your suggestion doesn't surprise me, Robin. This is all your fault. I've absolutely no doubt we'd have been invited to Balmoral if you hadn't kept chipping in with those snide little smutty little disgusting silly offensive dirty-minded camp quips. She can really influence things and what do you do? Go out of your way to create a bad impression, like a schoolkid writing rude words on the blackboard to shock teacher. It's what stops us earning acceptance, this jeering at everything decent and respectable. Well, if gays never get to take their partners to the Palace ball, it'll be your fault. Honestly, Robin, sometimes I wonder why I put up with you, you're so bloody immature."

It crossed my mind to stroke my crotch and say in an earthy voice, "You know why you put up with me," but I didn't think a snide little smutty little disgusting silly offensive dirty-minded camp quip would help.

While I discovered how distressed I was Dennis banged about in the kitchen washing up breakfast things. Then he returned as if he realised he had a mission to help people out of holes.

He said, "I apologise for what I said, Robin. I wasn't thinking straight. Actually, the Queen is on our side."

I was too repentant to ask how he made that out.

He coaxed, "Look, the Queen doesn't know we've no problems with it being publicly known we're gay, does she?"

"No." Dragged out, to show I couldn't see what was coming.

"She'll know our jobs and goodness knows what else could be at risk if there's publicity. And the newspapers all have these royal watchers spying on Balmoral and Buckingham Palace all the time, watching who's coming and going. So not mentioning us in the statement to the press, not risking exposing us by having us to Balmoral - it just shows her sympathy for the plight of gays. So you've nothing to feel bad about."

I jumped on board his train of thought. "If there'd been any mention of anyone helping her, the Press would have wheeled it out, who we were."

"Oh yes. Palace officials are terribly leaky." He spoke with knowledge born of years in Court circles.

"And what brought out this sympathy in her? Obviously, you bringing home to her how decent and respectable we can be."

This made Dennis smile so radiantly that I risked, "Tea and sympathy...they don't go together after all. Royal sympathy means no tea at Balmoral."

"I'll write and thank her for her delicate consideration. I don't think that would seem patronising."

THE KREUTZER SONATA

Carrying a violin-case, she limps into Philip's sitting-room. On each limp her long plait of grey hair jerks. On each limp, too, she says, "Fuck." She says it, Philip judges, automatically, because a pattern has been set up: limp, *fuck*; limp, *fuck*; limp, *fuck*. She doesn't know she's swearing.

She halts by the grand piano that dominates the room. "The minister's lovely wife is always available to assist a promising young musician in the parish."

She turns to scrutinise Philip. Her face takes on the cunning look of someone who has tumbled to a secret being kept from her. "The meeting for the buggers is in the minister's study."

"No, Catherine," coos the Reverend Moira Dinnett, as though the old lady had made the most natural mistake in the world. "Philip isn't one of the…" She swallows the last word. "Mr Boyes is the kind gentleman who was so sorry you couldn't play your violin in Fynloch Lodge and said I could bring you to play with him. He is an *excellent* pianist."

As if you'd know, Philip thinks. At that point his mobile rings and when he sees who it is he is nothing but need, almost out the door before he says, "Excuse me, I'll just take this in the hall."

"I got your text," Philip hears in the hall.

"Thank you."

"All right. We'll talk. Get it over with. I'll come round right away." Already, Philip is telling the old lady and Moira they must leave at once, *this instant*, it was the hospital, a relative mown down by a car, sorry, maybe we can re-arrange...

"Not now," Philip replies. It is definitely heroic, how right conduct, forgotten when Philip saw who the call was from, has now re-asserted itself; though, of course, things turn out well for people who do the right thing. "She's just arrived. The old lady, the violinist who's not allowed to play her violin in her care home. I *told* you."

That he can not only honour his appointment with the old lady but even imply criticism of Malcolm for forgetting shows that Philip is definitely not needy, oh no. He adds hopefully, "She'll be away by eight."

"Because of the buses I'll need to hang outside your place for around forty minutes," says Malcolm, as though the inconvenient bus service were another of Philip's failings. "Symbolic. I'm always hanging around. Until your family let go of you long enough to allow you to fit me in. You're 37! Think about that while you're tickling the ivories. I was always second fiddle."

"Thank you, thank you."

"You placed too much on me. Expected me to be an entire new family. I am not substitute father, mother, sister, brother."

"You're right, you're right," says Philip, exhilarated because there would be no point in Malcolm's saying all these things again unless as a prelude to giving their relationship another go, break-up rescinded. And note the encouraging present-tense of that *I'm always hanging around.*

The door to the sitting-room has opened a crack and closed again. "Right, see you at eight," he says heartily.

The door opens a crack again. "You're finished," Moira whispers, informatively, but also as though she might still be interrupting. She slips into the hall, shutting the door behind her. "I wanted a word before you came back through. I think she thought for a moment she was back in the manse and someone was trying to find a meeting. The memory for people and so on, the short-term memory, is all over the place. She can be a bit of a potty-mouth, too. But she'll be all right. Deep down she knows exactly why she's here, and I know she's *very* grateful."

How do you know? he thinks, then is surprised by a huge surge of anger on behalf of all oppressed people everywhere. This awful treatment of a helpless old woman by awful Fynloch Lodge, denying her what's most precious to her! He pictures the place going up in vengeful flames, though is scrupulous to script a safe transfer of all the residents to a nicer alternative.

He leads the way back into the sitting-room, away from the anger. "You'd think," he says with a calm maturity Malcolm must think well of, "there'd be a day-room, some out-of-the-way corner where she, you could play the violin."

Catherine Mackie stands just where she was before.

"Well," says Moira, professionally seeing both sides, "I suppose it could be a disturbance, people living in these little rooms, no sound insulation, everything done on the cheap. And some of the old ones can be a bit snappy." She lowers her voice in token inaudibility. "It was the cheapest home we could find. Alec didn't leave her much. She just sits in her chair all day staring…" Normal vocal service is resumed. "But when I heard that in our own congregation there was a real, trained pianist, I couldn't help trying to arrange *something* for you, Catherine."

"It will be a pleasure to play with you." Malcolm would approve of that, too. "I don't know how I'd cope if I couldn't play the piano."

She doesn't acknowledge this remark. She hangs on to her violin-case as Moira helps her off with her coat. There's a stain, pure care-home, on the front of her limp floral-patterned dress. When Moira makes as if to undo the violin-case, the old lady whisks it away with surprising energy and takes out the violin herself. Without change of personnel in Philip's sitting-room, someone arrives. Catherine plays a few notes, manipulates the pegs that tune the instrument. Philip plays the A she needs for tuning. She opens the score of the Kreutzer Sonata he's placed on a music stand for her and murmurs, "Ah, the Henle Urtext edition."

She announces, "The minister's lovely wife makes a long-awaited return to the concert platform."

"Ready?" says Philip.

He learns that she is indeed ready, though he could not say whether it was from a flicker of her eyes or a barely-perceptible nod. She begins the slow sequence of chords for violin alone that opens the first movement.

The sound is in quest of something, there is uncertainty in it.

Oh dear.

With a leap of the heart Philip realises that the questing and the uncertainty are entirely within the music, not at all in the performer. He plays the answering sequence for piano alone without thought of her age and infirmity, and the ensuing dialogue of two-note phrases between the two instruments establishes a bond of trust between them that allows the subsequent *Presto* to take off with exhilarating brio.

"Oh, excellent," cries Moira like a primary school teacher inducing self-esteem, and without missing a beat or a note Catherine growls, "Quiet, you silly!" Philip grins to himself: he and the old lady have forged an alliance in music and in other things, too. Everything is going to be all right - at least, as far as the music is concerned.

As regards Malcolm, who knows?

For all its difficulty, the rest of the first movement fulfils the promise of a happy collaboration: they are nothing but two dedicated musicians losing and so freeing themselves in their music. Its two concluding chords, in perfect unison, express the triumph of her undiminished ability and hopefully presage a different triumph for Philip after eight o'clock.

"The lavatory." Catherine lays her violin on the piano.

"Oh, yes, of course...I'll just show you." Philip leads her into the hall. There's no swearing now. He's proud that their music-making restored her to normality. He indicates the lavatory door, moves to open it for her.

"This is something in which I need no assistance whatsoever." That could have given lessons in rebuking to Lady Bracknell, but then Catherine peers at Philip in her secret-fathoming way again. "What are you doing in this part of the house? The meeting for the buggers is in my husband's study downstairs."

Philip retreats to the sitting-room.

"She's good," he tells Moira.

"Well, she could have had a professional career, she won prizes at the Academy, everyone said she was brilliant, but—"

"She's a *wonderful* player." For a moment there he forgot Malcolm.

"—but, well, Alec's career always came first and she just followed him around."

"That's a *travesty!*" He is so familiar both with the phenomenon of family members crushing the life-blood

out of you and with the modern mis-use of *travesty* in
which it is curiously shorn of anything to be a travesty *of.*

"It was what women did. The husband's career was
what was important. And a minister's wife was expected to
be the minister's full-time unpaid assistant. Sometimes
there'd be some part-time school-teaching, perhaps some
local amateur players to play with, but.... It didn't help
that Alec was so outspoken in support of, you know,
lesbians and gays"—does she sound like someone trying to
be non-alarmist about a diagnosis of cancer?—"in the Kirk
at a time when hardly anyone else was; one of the
newspapers called him the *poofs' pastor.* I did my final
placement with him when I was training, and people
looked at *me!*" She laughs heartily. "He tended to get out-
of-the-way parishes where no-one else wanted to go.
Difficult ones. She was never on the spot long enough in
somewhere like Glasgow or Edinburgh to build a musical
career. Sometimes, down in the Borders, she'd play in
orchestras for amateur musicals just for the pleasure of
performing with other musicians. Way below her level.
Hello Dolly! and things."

"Really, she's completely out of my league," says Philip.

He has used the same phrase of Malcolm.

They hear her limp along the hall. The accompanying
swearing seems to be back, but Philip can't make out the
word.

"Sh, here she is," says Moira.

Limp, *buggers*; limp, *buggers*; limp, *buggers*.

"Drawing attention to themselves," she says severely.
"Here in a hospital."

"No, no," Moira soothes. "This isn't the hospital.
Catherine had an operation - didn't you, Catherine?—and
two of the male nurses were rather, well, I think the word

is *camp*—and they had a double act, I suppose you'd call it, that many of the patients found very entertaining. They cheered people up, which can be so important in hospital, but let's just say that they weren't Catherine's cup of tea. Were they, Catherine? But this isn't the hospital. It's Philip's flat!"

To resurrect the musician and sweep away the alarming possibility that he has a manner that reminds Catherine of the camp pair at the hospital, Philip plays the theme that begins the second movement. It's gentle, almost dreamy, and there's a defiant pleasure in imagining it as 'our tune' for himself and Malcolm, though first he'd need to change Malcolm's musical tastes. The sound of the piano does what he hoped, silences the old lady, refocuses her, and the violin entry comes just where it should. They unwind the andante in perfect yearning amity.

"That's lovely," calls Moira.

Catherine says something - a reply to Moira?

Philip realises it is again *buggers*. She emits it from time to time. When 'our tune' begins its first variation she calls *buggers* in time to the high triplets on C that feature in the violin's part, *buh-uh-ggers*. She calls it with a kind of mad cheerful trilling lightness.

Things take a more manic turn in the second variation, where the violin part unfolds in continuous sequences of four fast notes, papapapa, papapapa, papapapa, papapapa. Though it's too fast for her to utter the plural, *buggers*, from the start she utters a syllable to every note, *buggerbugger, buggerbugger, buggerbugger, buggerbugger.*

But her voice soon becomes sound without meaning, an idling motor easily overridden by the unimpaired deftness and grace of her violin.

During the later variations her words are no longer

confined to *buggers*. "Disgusting, disgusting, disgusting, disgusting, disgusting," she chants, and then, "Buggers in the hospital, buggers in the hospital," and then, "Drawing attention, drawing attention, drawing attention." There's no attempt now to fit the words to the music, and they're so loud and emphatic and persistent that they resist blanking out. The present-tense of Malcolm's *I'm always hanging around* is obliterated by the irrevocable past tense of his *I was always second fiddle* and *You placed too much on me*. Philip's fingers alone, not his heart, take him to the end of the second movement. *Get it over with.*

Moira claps enthusiastically, perhaps a retrospective attempt to drown out Catherine's words. "Not finished," Catherine orders, without so much as a glance at her.

Philip's hands are between his knees. It is evident that Malcolm is making his bus journey only because he has the good manners to complete the ending of their relationship face to face, the relationship that he, Philip, shipwrecked by all the awful ways in which he was alternately distant and clinging.

He stares at the keyboard, aware that Catherine is waiting for him to sound the loud A major chord that begins the whirling last movement.

Beethoven changed the dedication of this piece from the violinist he was originally going to dedicate it to because the man made a smutty remark about a lady of Beethoven's acquaintance. Good old heaven-storming Beethoven, fiery, standing up for his principles, refusing to take his hat off to the emperor. Wouldn't it be following in Beethoven's footsteps over this very piece, if Philip refused to carry on playing it with someone uttering such vile words that besmirch Malcolm?

Philip looks up to fathom the hatred in Catherine's eyes

and finds nothing but the focused eye of the musician, all ego absent, patiently awaiting his concurrence in the renewal of their musical communion. And before he knows it - against his will, it feels - he's walloped (but musically!) the A major chord and she's launched the violin into the helter-skelter tarantella that dominates the movement and produces out of nowhere an expanding delight. He and Catherine might be dancing together, blending and twining and circling round each other, pain all gone.

She's talking again, chanting, singing, fitting it to the tarantella rhythm, even to its tune: "Sodomites, sodomites, sodomites, gay! Sodomites, sodomites, sodomites, gay!"

He fights off his anger, tells himself it's just a tic, a verbal tic, and finds that in his head he, too, is fitting words to the tarantella: "It's just a tic, it's just a tic, it's just a tic, a tic! It's just a tic, it's just a tic, it's just a tic, a tic!"

"Catherine!" Moira calls in entirely good-natured sing-song. "You'll put Philip off!"

She certainly doesn't put herself off. You could believe her violin is animated by Beethoven's score alone, without any intermediary, let alone a fallible human one. The notes, the rhythm, every nuance of phrasing - all are perfectly in place. There's no faltering, even when, seemingly triggered by Moira's reproof, she recommences her unrhythmic chanting: "Buggers in my husband's study, disgusting, disgusting, buggers in the hospital, disgusting, drawing attention, drawing attention, disgusting, disgusting, sodomites, sodomites, get out, get out, get out, burn, burn, burn at the stake, buggers, buggers, buggers, my husband's study, disgusting, sodomites, sodomites…"

Just imagine a demon has bored a hole through her brain, making a speaking-tube to broadcast his invective.

It's not coming from her. The wonderful musician is her.

No!

This is not, after all, a matter of words gabbled automatically, without meaning. These are clusters of related phrases the old hag is spewing. They add up. She can't be unaware of what they mean. They manifest understanding and intent and a dark hatred for Philip and his kind. Philip *must* defy this abuse; for his life's sake; for Malcolm's sake; for the sake of everything true and lovely Malcolm has shown him but that he has lost forever. He will cry "No!" He will halt. He will rise to his feet and slam down the lid over the keys.

And all the while his distress, his determination to halt, his positive decision to halt *this very second* - these exist in some separate and irrelevant region of himself, imprisoned there by the music that makes him its unresisting channel and his hands its unwavering servants. The pure stream issuing from her violin is magnified into an immensely potent kindness, drawing out of Philip abilities he didn't know he had. A dozen or so bars from the end there's a high right-hand trill above low triplets in the left hand, and he's never managed this before without a slight but unfortunate slackening of speed, but this time Catherine's own trill in the same bars carries him along with her at her own rollicking tempo. He's safely into the final joyous dash of his fingers down the board to the united A that is so plainly the end that Moira can clap without fear of reproof. "Bravo, bravo," she calls. "Oh, now wasn't that something? Marvellous, absolutely marvellous."

Catherine bows, but not towards Moira. For a moment Philip thinks she's honouring him, and notwithstanding *buggers* and *sodomites* and *disgustings*, the words reforming themselves in his consciousness in all their venom, and notwithstanding the final doom heading his way this very moment with Malcolm, he exults.

But, no, she's obviously not bowing to him, either. The audience to whom she is bowing, again and again, is somewhere else, remembered, imaginary, perhaps what once was dreamed of.

"The minister's lovely wife has not shamed Max Rostal," she says.

Moira throws Philip a look saying that he, too, must be wondering what that means.

The cunning look comes back into Catherine's eyes.

She puts her violin to her chin again and begins to play. Philip is intent on identifying something from the classical repertoire—a Bach partita for solo violin, a Paganini caprice? Only when Moira, her face radiant with having a good time, begins to sing along does he recognise it.

…see you back where you belong.

You're lookin' swell, Dolly.

I can tell, Dolly

Surreptitiously he edges his shirt-sleeve back. Seven o'clock. An hour until he knows whether he will be back where he belongs.

There is nothing for him to do but sing along, too.

You're still glowin', you're still crowin',

You're still goin' strong.

You could say that about Catherine, too, at least as regards her violin.

Philip's voice and Moira's take on increasing gusto.

…Find her an empty lap, fellas

Dolly'll never go away again!

A cup of tea before she leaves? But Catherine begins the tune again, ornaments it. There are slides upwards and downwards, a wild gypsy spin, jazz inflexions, a bluesy melisma. Suddenly it's metamorphosed into a version of the rondo tune from the last movement of the Beethoven Violin Concerto, and the melody of *Hello, Dolly!* - now left to their voices alone - somehow sits on top of it as comfortably as Dolly on an empty lap.

Perhaps the violin and the voices can be heard in the street outside, in the city where at this very moment in a hospital ward the two camp nurses may be performing their double act, amusing patients and making them feel better; where other women are no doubt regretting lost lives and other pupils of the great Max Rostal may be looking ruefully at arthritic fingers; and where on a bus south of the river Malcolm is getting closer with an expression on his face that Philip tries to read and that he finally interprets as meaning that, like Dolly, Malcolm will never go away again.

God's Own Country

I saved Judy Garland by taking her hill-walking in Scotland.

See, in those days we didn't fall in love with each other in Glasgow. Oh, the guys would have, you know, sex with each other, but to *really* fall in *love*...well, you'd, like, go down to London, you could meet *fantastic* guys down there, and there were places you could actually dance together, too. And someone would come back and say he'd met this great guy, and they'd try to keep it going, him going down to London at weekends. Sometimes the London guy might actually come up here. But usually it fizzled out after a bit—the distance and so on.

Well, I went down for a weekend, and, yes, I met this guy, Jude. Really good-looking he was, dark hair, great dresser, really knew his way around, he had everything together. Fantastic guy, he was. So I thought. Actually, his name was James, James Fairfax-Vere, but he called himself Jude because of that Beatles song, *Hey, Jude*. I met him in this pub I'd been told about and he came up and talked, so friendly, like he'd known I'd be there and he'd come there just to meet me, and he said, Wherever you thought you were going to stay tonight, forget it. You're staying with me. I'll make sure you enjoy it. When he said that he just stared at me and his eyes, you know, compelled me. Not that I didn't want to—I mean, I couldn't believe my luck. And he was a fabulous lover, just taking his time, I'd never experienced anything like it. In the past it had all been getting down to it right away, you know, getting your thrill.

And after it was over he said, I'm very glad I've got you into my life, Tommy, I just know we're going to spend a lot of time together, and he tapped me on the nose, playful.

The next weekend I decided to surprise him so I 'phoned in sick at work and caught the coach down and got to his place—a really fantastic flat—on the Friday night, and I went up the stairs and rang the bell, and when he answered he didn't seem to know who I was, and I said, jokey, Remember me? It's lover-boy. And he didn't seem to know what to say, and I was standing there, smiling at him, and I was wanting him to, you know, take me in his arms, and a couple of times he started to say something and stopped, and then he said, Well, it's awfully sweet of you to look in, Billy, and then he said, Off to somewhere nice, are you? And I said I'd come to see *him*, and I thought, you know, nothing ventured, and I said it, just like that, "I love you, Jude."

And he said, That's good, that's good, so long as we all love each other, what else matters, all you need is love, hey? But he just stood there and just sort of smiled, and it was a nothing smile. And I asked him, wasn't he going to ask me in, and he said, and he sounded really sorry as he said it, Billy, I *am* sorry, I *really* am, but I've got some dreadful party to go to.

He just stood there saying nothing with that nothing smile, and I could see there was nothing more to be said, and I said, Bye for now, and he said, Ciao. And he watched me go down the stairs and gave me a little wave, which meant something, I suppose, and shut the door.

Well, I was really disappointed, but when I got down the stairs I thought I'd try again, because I loved him. And after last weekend, the previous weekend, I *knew* there was a really nice guy there, I knew he really liked me, if I could just get through to him. So I thought I'd go back and say I'd just wait there in the flat, and he could go out and I'd be waiting for him when he came back. And if he came back with someone else, well, he had the right to do that, I didn't want to put any pressure on him, I'd just slip away. So I went back up but as I was going to knock I could hear his voice, he was on the 'phone, and I heard him say, Guess who has just turned up, my little gap-toothed piece of Glaswegian rough. And he said I was awfully sweet in a way but not something you went back to, and anyway Adam, I think it was, was back. And I don't mind saying I went back down the stairs and when he couldn't hear me just sat down on the carpet and had a greet. And I didn't know where I was going to go.

But then I thought he might come out to go to his party and find me there, and I wasn't going to have that, I've got my pride, so I got up and went out the door and stood on the pavement wondering what to do, it was just getting dark, and then suddenly this little woman came running along and banged into me, and she shouted, Get out of the way, motherfucker. And then she stopped and just stood there, not looking at me, just staring nowhere, and then her face sort of went, collapsed, and it was like she was in agony, all alone in agony, and she said in this really terrible voice, not saying it *to* anyone, Oh, what am I going to do? It was Judy Garland.

And I asked her, trying to be gentle and show respect, What is it, hen? And what she said was this: "I've killed her." And then she came out of her nowhere stare and sort of *saw* me, and she said in this pleading way, I don't know who you are, mister, but you look nice. Please help me.

Well, I couldn't resist that, and she was sobbing now,

and I put my arm round her shoulders and said, Tell me all about it, I'll do anything I can to help, and she looked at me, but she didn't quite believe me yet, and she said, Will you? And it was the most fantastic story. She said she had this double, Ethel Hotchkiss, that they used for Judy in films, and this Ethel knew an awful lot about Judy, about pills and booze and drugs and bad stuff, and she'd been blackmailing Judy. And she'd actually been up to Judy's place that night trying to get money out of her—Judy's husband then, Mickey Deans, had gone out because they'd had a blazing row about something. And then this Ethel told Judy that if she told what she knew Judy's never get her career up off the skids. Well, Judy didn't know what to do, she thought she'd have to pay up like she always did, and then she had an idea—she'd slip this Ethel something that would knock her out till Mickey came back and he could deal with her, and she gave her this drink which she'd slipped all sorts of pills and things into. Well, she'd overdone it. Ethel got ill and went to the bathroom and didn't come out and after a bit Judy sort of peeked in and there was Ethel *dead*! And now Judy was hugging me like I was her only hope and I had to protect and save her.

And then it came to me, I *could* save her. I told her, Look, Judy, if that woman's your double, this is the chance you've been waiting for. You can *really* change your life, cut loose from all your troubles. I mean, I know how it's been for you, I read the papers. But they'll think this Ethel is you, that it's Judy that's dead. So there's an end to all the pressure, and you can start your life again, quietly, and change your name, and put all the dramas and suicide attempts and pills and booze and stuff behind you and come and live with me in Glasgow, I stay by myself.

She looked a bit doubtful, so I said, It's the perfect

solution. But she still didn't say anything, she just hugged me the more, like she was a kid, really, and I said, When we get to Scotland we'll go up in the hills, go hill-walking. I can show you fantastic places and views, I'd love to do that, and it'll be so good for you, the air, exercise, get all the booze and pills and pain out of your system, you'll be *happy* at last.

And she looked up and made a decision, and she just said, "Okay, I'll try anything, I can't fight any more."

*　　*　　*

It was a fantastic day in early May, spring, the best time for the hills, and I drove us in the van down Glen Etive, it's all sort of crowded in with big pointy hills with steep sides. And I was planning for us to go up Ben Starav, this massive hill right on the sea's edge, you see it and you think, Christ, it goes up and *up*. But actually it doesn't take that long, there's a clear path, and the view from the top knocks you out, the top is a sort of plateau with, like, two horns, one on each side, absolutely unmistakable. But Judy just took one look—I carried the big rucksack, she had just a little one—and she said, You're crazy, I can't go up there. She'd put on shorts, blue ones, her legs were a bit white and podgy, and a headscarf and dark glasses.

I said, Yes, you can, Judy.

Then she started shouting and screaming, there at the roadside where I'd parked the van between some gorse bushes. She really lost the rag. I was a brute and a monster, she just *couldn't*, I was driving her mad, I was another fucking man fucking up her life, who did I think I was, all that kind of stuff. I grabbed her wrists and then got them into one hand, and all the time I was telling her, Judy, it's for your own good, you've *got* to do this, you'll prove to yourself that you *can* change and get out of your old ways and be on the road to happiness. She was squirming and resisting, but I had her wrists firm and then with my free hand I hit her across the face, twice, just two wee controlled slaps, really, like they do to hysterical women in films, and at once she quietened down and changed completely, and in that kind of strong voice of hers that made you feel you could really rely on her, for anything, she said, Okay, Tommy, let's go.

So off we go, and to cheer her along I talk about this and that, and it really works. I tell her something I've read somewhere that someone called Deirdre of the Sorrows lived in Glen Etive once, and she says, I've had a few sorrows myself, and I say, But they're going to be over soon just like April showers, and she gives me such a real warm smile. She asks me about Deirdre of the Sorrows, and I don't know much, but I tell her I think she was an Irish princess hundreds of years ago who was forced to be married to some Scottish prince who lived in the glen, and then probably she had to take her husband's part in a war against her own folks and all her brothers were killed or something, and we stop, already we're high up, and look down at the long narrow loch running into the glen from the sea, and we imagine, you know, long ships like Viking boats sailing up under the mountains all those hundreds of years ago, and Deirdre standing by the mast staring out, and Judy says, "Poor damn kid."

On up we go, it's steep but no problem if you take it steady, and then something really nice happens. For God's sake, look at that, she says, and I look and she's looking at a beer can someone has pressed down between two rocks—the path goes over lots of loose rocks—and she says, Why do they have to leave their frigging beer cans up here and spoil God's own country? And she says, Do you know what really gets me?—they think if they crush the damn thing with their boot first it isn't a fucking eyesore, God, sometimes I despair of people. I'm thinking, that's a good sign, she *cares* about the mountain and not spoiling things, and that means she's mending. And then she says, "But not you, Tommy."

And so we reach the top, it's a big area and we wander about looking at the view, there's this other hill across the loch with these sort of huge black slabs hundreds of feet high running down the sides, and everything is so tiny in the glen, it's so far below, and the sun is shining and everything is, like, clean and new and bright and vast, and there's still bits of snow here and there on the hills, and it's so white and shining like it was your heart's desire and you have this big ache to reach out to it across miles, and you see clouds, shadows of them, moving across the glen and other hills, and we have this fantastic feeling that it's good, actually *good*, to be alive, and I say, she being American, Freaks you out, doesn't it? And she takes my hand and looks at me serious and says, Tommy, you've *given* this to me, and if it wasn't for you I'd never have seen it, and it's all so real, and I can see it, really *see* it, and I'm sort of part of it, and, oh, I feel so much *peace* inside, and how can I ever thank you enough? I don't mind saying I'm in tears.

And then we find a couple of rocks as seats and we eat our food and I've brought a thermos of coffee and Judy's really enjoying herself, she says, This is the best goddam doughnut I have ever eaten in my whole goddam life, and jam sort of squirts out on to her chin, and we both laugh, and I think, I really have saved her.

And then she says something odd, but in a very ladylike

way, very delicate. She says, Tommy, ever since we came up to Glasgow on the coach and I came to live with you, you've never, well, Tommy, there doesn't seem to be a lady-friend in your life.

No, I say, and I feel a bit awkward.

Tommy, she says, I don't want you to alter your life for me. I mean, if you're keeping her away because you think I'd mind, well, I know it's only a little flat but I wouldn't think my privacy was being invaded if you, you know, invited her up.

And I say, It's not like that, Judy. You see, I'm gay, the word was coming in.

At this she bursts out laughing in a way I didn't like, a bit of the old Judy returning, and she says, God, a fruit. I didn't like that. And she kept laughing. And then it, the laughing, became more friendly, and she says, Just like some of my frigging husbands, and she hugs me, and I hug her back, and we're laughing together now. And she says, Well, Tommy, I don't mind making tea for a gentleman-friend, either.

And I say, No, there's no-one now, I got hurt, and I think I'm best out of it, that sort of thing, love and so on. I'd rather have you as my friend, Judy.

Ben Starav is not a totally separate, separated hill. I mean, it's joined to others along a ridge. Next along from it is a hill called Glas Bheinn Mhor. Well, as we were sitting eating and chatting I could see this tiny figure coming along the ridge from this next hill, sometimes you could see it, like a tiny ant, sometimes not, and then it would be further on again. Well, I didn't really think about it, but then Judy went off to find a place to have a pee and I stood up and started wandering about again, just looking at the view and the drop and so on, when this little figure

I'd seen in the distance arrives at the top, and it's Jude Fairfax-Vere. And he says, all warm and friendly, Tommy, you're just the person I've been hoping to meet, I came up to Scotland specially to try to find you.

No problem, I tell him, you had my number.

Did I, he says, I must have lost it. Then he says, looking at me sort of meaningfully with those, you know, compelling eyes he had, You always lose the things you value most.

I say I don't follow him.

And he says, Look, Tommy, I want to apologise, I treated you bad, real bad, I'll never forgive myself for what I did to you.

I don't quite know what to say to this, but he doesn't look for any reply, and he says, What I've come to say, Tommy, is, I love you and I want to spend my life with you more than with anyone else. He thinks this is a compliment, but I think, Ah, so there's others in for the job, too. And he steps forward as if I'm going to fall into his arms right there on top of Ben Starav with all the forest and sea and sky all around. And I tell him, It's not as simple as that, and he looks surprised. Arrogant sod, assuming all he's got to do is snap his fingers and put on that awful smooth sincere English voice and I'll come running.

And he says, and now to look at his face you'd think he was genuinely hurt, like I'd been bad to *him*, Tommy, what have I done?

I'll tell you what you've done, says a voice, and there's Judy, back from doing what nobody could do for her. She says, You called the nicest, sweetest man in the whole frigging world a gap-toothed bit of Glaswegian rough and you threw him aside like a used Kleenex.

57

And he says, But, my God, I realise what a mistake I made, Tommy, don't you believe me? I love you, I'm desperate for you, I want you back.

But Judy says, It's too late for that. You hurt and damaged him and he doesn't want you messing him up again.

And now he ignores me and speaks to her. He says, Judy, when my father dies I shall be I shall be *Sir* James Fairfax-Vere, I shall inherit Fairfax Castle, in Suffolk or somewhere, he said. I invite you to share it with me, he says, a huge real castle, Judy, that's the setting for a star like you, not his Godforsaken hole of a city.

And now Judy gets really wild. She says, You lousy son of a bitch loser, you motherfucking English slimeball, get the hell out of here, let me tell you that not all the frigging faggotty Fairfax Castles and fucking titles in the whole goddam could *begin* to equal the happiness, the TRUE HAPPINESS, I've found with Tommy in our little flat in Glasgow. And she starts picking up rocks and throwing them at him, raging and screaming, and one hits him in the mouth, and I think, That'll do for your beautiful good looks for a bit, maybe break one of *your* teeth, you piss-elegant shite. And he turns and runs, with Judy still shouting and chucking rocks behind him, and the last we see of him he's hurrying back the way he came, along to Glas Bheinn Mhor.

And Judy is smiling, there's, like, absolute joy on her face, joy in absolutely everything, her face is, like, purified, and she links her arm in mine and says, Well, we saw him off, Tommy, if that's the man that got away, let him go. And now there's not a thing to stop us caring for each other and being happy. Oh, I know I've been a rotten frigging bitch sometimes, Tommy, but deep down I could see you were giving me what I've always needed in my life, and I want to tell you you're the greatest and grandest fella I've ever known.

Of course, we didn't have a lot of money, because she was supposed to be dead so we couldn't get at any of hers. But that didn't matter, we managed, and she said, I'd rather be happy with you, Tommy, than rich and miserable and screwed up like I used to be. And we had happy, happy times over the years. She had a stoke a while back, she recovered well but it left her a bit shaky and tottery, and she got old, into her nineties, and I couldn't afford to stop work and look after her because we only had my money, so she went into a, you know, home at Strathblane, and I go out every weekend to see her, and she's settled down there really well. The warden said a funny thing, she's quite young, just a lassie, really, but she wears these women's suits like Margaret Thatcher used to with a big bow in the front, they have karaoke nights at the home and Judy's still game for a song, she absolutely slays them, and this warden, she says, You're auntie's just like that Liza Minnelli.

CONTINUING CITY

The image I need is given me by the 'plane as it tilts down towards Glasgow. The vast carpet of lights by night is a jewelled Jerusalem, a wonder. But each light in that vast carpet is solitary and tiny. If it went out, the eye would not notice any difference in the great glittering sweep. And so the lives that go on down there are tiny solitary things, too, entirely dispensable, each of them a pin-prick of light that doesn't really count for anything.

I am about to try whether this image is the truth.

I have met Robert only once, and that was half a lifetime ago, in 1977. *Met*. Is that the right word for a one-night stand?

"Oh, a one-night stand. The perfect shorthand representation of the lack of meaningful human connection in big cities." That is the received opinion. Actually, I used to have another angle. I used to say, "Promiscuity is a way of taming the frightening hordes you pass in the streets. You don't know any of them, they've all got lives that are unknown to you, and God! they might be *better* lives than yours! Sleeping with them is way of cutting them down to size, of making sure that no-one else is happier than you are. Only another 863,471 Glaswegians to go—and I'm leaving the women till last."

I remember—what? Straight, very fine blondish hair that flopped about: he will go bald early. A comfortable looseness of flesh that was not quite fat. A cock that wouldn't unshrivel. A mouth that often bore a secret joyous smile accompanied by downcast eyes. Arms that held me and hugged me, again and again. Lots of smacking puckered-lip kisses. His attempt, as he riffled through my records, to pronounce "Schütz", and, when I corrected him, his sweet look that said: that's another important thing mastered. Oh yes, and although he seemed absolutely artless and open there was a core to him that was separate from everything I could see or hear or touch, like an invisible altar.

I did not suggest meeting again, and though I probably said (for I usually said it), "See you around," I didn't. There were moments when I thought of him; for instance, at a club where the dancers looked over their partners' shoulders to see what other possibilities might be about.

Then at Christmas came a card from him. It was signed just "Robert", no surname and no address, but I knew it was from him because although at that point I had worked my way through ninety-four Glaswegians, none of the others had been called Robert; at least, going by what they told me.

There were three crosses for kisses. One would have meant nothing, a mere formality, but three endearingly indicated a gush of puppylike love.

The name on the envelope puzzled me at first: "Mark Down"—correct forename, which I'd told him, but wrong surname. There'd been no call to give my surname. Then I realised what had happened: I'd only just bought the flat when I brought Robert back, Down was the surname of the old lady who'd lived there before and died, and the brass plate with her name on it had still been at the door. For all his inexperience, he'd been canny enough to memorise the name-plate and address.

But then, perhaps he wouldn't have done that if he'd not been inexperienced.

In 1978 his card added a surname in brackets, McHugh, and the address of a flat in Govan. Ah, he had come out to his parents, he could now afford to give his surname and address. No kisses this year, but these three words in large, loopy, painstaking handwriting: "Thanks for everything." That had no application to me, but it was touching that he wanted to put in a personal message; touching, too, that he was too clumsy to come up with an appropriate one.

I sent back a card, writing just "Mark".

This produced, two months later, a Valentine card. The front had a cartoon sketch of a man riffling through stacks of gramophone records, and it bore the words, "I remember all my old favourites, but best of all..." When you opened it, the words continued, "...I remember you." This allusion to the Frank Ifield hit from his childhood showed there was something constant in him that had not been overthrown by the passing invasions of punk and disco music. He had written, "Love, Robert."

So he was now sufficiently at ease with himself to send a Valentine card to another man, and that without a hint of jokiness or camp. That was another sign of integrity.

I did not respond to Robert's Valentine. I was seeing Stephen, and things were getting serious. Still, Robert's card had its effect. It emboldened me to start living with Stephen, for if things went wrong with Stephen—well, Robert was like money in the bank you've only just discovered is there.

As for me and Stephen, that is the subject of an entirely different story, one that takes place wholly above ground in the daylight. It is a story of complete love, unqualified happiness. I am stunned with wonder when I think of it.

That year there was no Christmas card from Robert,

nor the next. Just the natural fading-out of contact between people who are getting on with their lives, moving on? (People who speak of 'moving on' usually refer to the jettisoning of some person who has meant something to you.) Oh no, this was pure pique, because I'd not responded to his Valentine. I can see the sulky look on that slightly too fleshy face: all right, be like that, I won't speak to *you*, either. When Stephen and I flew home from our first holiday in Key West and the 'plane circled in over the city—this was in daylight so I had no shining nocturnal sweep to muse on as I had before the descent tonight—I tried to locate Govan in the shifting panorama below me, for in Govan there stood, invisible to everyone but me, a tall transmitter like in the old trademark for RKO movies. It radiated pulses of sullen resentment in all directions, and our 'plane was just coming into receiving range.

There wasn't another card until 1982, and it was meant to put my nose out of joint. There were no kisses, no love, just two names intimately linked by an ampersand: "Nigel & Robert." *So there!*

The style of card had changed, too. It was no longer the large tacky glitter-covered kind of card with slushy verse that had been Robert's natural choice. This one had some Baroque Italian Madonna-and-child on the cover and was sold in aid of Shelter. Robert had been taken in hand, was being given some of the class he'd always wanted. "Nigel" is an unusual name in Scotland. I could see how a well-spoken Englishman, a bit older, with his own elegant flat, could be attractive to a boy from Govan; vice-versa, too.

There was no address so I couldn't send a card back. Having made his point, Robert sent no card for the next three years. Oh, he's hard in his resentments, is Robert.

But early in 1986, amid all the waiting junk mail when Stephen and I get back from skiing in Austria, is an envelope addressed in Robert's handwriting. I hide the envelope as though it's a guilty secret, and in fact I read it sitting on the lavatory, and I even lock the door, which is something Stephen and I did not normally do, though I lock it quietly so that he will not know.

Dear Mark,

I hope you do'nt mind me writing, its just that I have'nt really got anyone else, all our friends are Nigels. Nigel and I seem to be falling apart, just my luck.

Oh, the fatalism of the boy from Govan who doesn't think things can ever go right for him! I think of the transient miracle of his functioning body, bestowed on some emotionally-crippled Englishman who can't recognise an honest loving heart, and I shake my head.

I get pretty depressed, it makes me think of all the other mistakes I made.

But *he* hasn't made any mistakes.

Nigel wants this David to come and live with us, he say's hes just a lodger, but I know better. Nigel say's he needs a place to live because he went and got tested for this AIDS and something got sent to his home and his parents threw him out, although it was negative. What Im writing for is not to hassle you with my problems, I know Ive got to face them on my own, but to ask you if you know anywhere I can rent to live, cheap? Hoping to hear from you, Robert.

If he needs to find somewhere to live, there are plenty of shop windows that carry adverts on cards. What he is really asking is: am I free, can we be lovers?

I had to knock that hope on the head, though it was irrelevant to mention Stephen. I wrote back:

> *Dear Robert,*
> *I was sorry to hear about your problems and hope things are working out. Sorry, I don't know of anyone with a room to let.*

I didn't think there could be any harm in attempting a bit of comfort:

> *Remember, it might be all as Nigel says, nothing for you to worry about. You were always a romantic—I remember you singing* **Strangers in the Night** *to me in 1977, the line about "in love forever"—and it's because you are a romantic that you might imagine problems where there aren't any.*

I wasn't sure how to end it. "Yours" was obviously out of the question. "Take care" was too much like a brush-off. In the end I settled for, "Take care, Robert," the use of the name giving permissible weight and concern.

But I could feel his disappointment. I went and copied down some addresses from a shop window in Byres Road and put them in with the letter.

Next Christmas he wrote in his big glittery card: "Thanks a million. Fantastic flat." The Gibson Street address he gave was one of the ones I'd sent him. And the card was signed, "Robert & David," with a shameless ampersand!

The sly clever bugger! That would teach that Nigel to play games with my Robert. I rushed to the 'phone book, and, yes, there was a number for him at the flat in Gibson Street. Of course, I didn't telephone. But the fact that a telephone wire ran between my house and his was breathtaking.

I'd almost not got that card. I found it lying on our hall table where we put letters to go to the post. It was addressed, as usual, to Mark Down, and Stephen had written "Not known", prior to putting it back in the post. When I said the first name might have made him think it was for me his face suggested a penny only just dropping. But the next two years were, I think, the best of all our wonderful years together.

These were years in which deaths were becoming more frequent, and when no card came in 1988, I feared the obvious. We were told we shouldn't speak of *victims* of AIDS, but poor loving Robert would have been a victim all right—victim of two-faced David's slimy secret infidelities.

All was explained next year, though. "The business is really taking off. We spent last Christmas in the Bahamas and did'nt send a single card. Sorry!"

Neither then nor previously nor in any subsequent card was there any other mention of the business. This was significant. It showed I was someone Robert thought about a lot: his thoughts flew magnetically to me at all sorts of times and junctures. He was so used to talking to me in his mind that he forgot he'd told me nothing about the business in reality.

The card next year arrived before the end of November. This was significant, too. The card announced a change of address. Obviously he didn't want to risk not getting my card. It mattered to him that a card my hands had touched, signed, placed in its envelope, should find its way across the city and end up between his fingers.

I suppose someone might think that these cards dominated my years, that the years were nothing to me but the before and after of my exchange of cards with Robert at Christmas. That is not at all the case. I had a full life going on in the real world, in the daylight, in which I didn't give a thought to Robert and his cards from one year's end to the next. I left my council job and trained as a teacher, Stephen became a partner in a law firm, we lived through the Poll Tax and the Gulf War in 1991, Stephen's sister was murdered....

They—for it was still "Robert & David"—now lived in Kelvin Court in Great Western Road, a classy address: the business was indeed doing well. Of course, it was all Robert's doing, his drive and acumen that fired it. David, small and dark-haired with uneasy eyes, incapable of applying himself to anything, lived off Robert.

One dark rainy evening I'd been to Helensburgh to leave a present for Stephen with his parents in advance of the special dinner we always had with them on the anniversary of our first meeting. Driving back I was on a high of joy about my life with Stephen, actually smiling. I pulled into the car park at Kelvin Court.

I sat there for a time with the engine off. I looked up at the great proud 1930s blocks of flats with their jutting wings. High up inside were Robert and David. At the door would be a set of bell-pushes with illuminated little frames for occupants' names, and I tried to imagine Robert's surname conjoined with another: McHugh Brodie, McHugh Jenkins, McHugh Watson. I realised these were all real Davids I had known.

I got out and went to what looked like a main entrance.

There were numbers and bell-pushes but no frames for

occupants' names. Really classy places didn't have them, I supposed. Still, I let a magnetic force draw my thumb to Robert's bell-push, and I rested it there, too gently for the bell to sound. I felt in my thumb a faint electric pulse that I could send bursting into Robert's flat, into his unknown world.

"Just passing, thought I'd look you up," I could say. But what was the point? The connection we had could not be more real just because of the irrelevant particularities of presence, spoken words, flesh, clasped hands.

There was some kind superintendent's office adjoining the entrance. It was lighted and I thought I caught a movement. I pictured someone weighted with the authority of all the money in Kelvin Court coming out and asking me my business there: what could I say? So I hurried away, and drove off in the rain, and Robert would never know I had stood there with my thumb on the bell-push.

Things like that happen all the time in cities and no-one knows about them.

Although with Stephen I had the happiness one dreams of, nevertheless there are people who will understand that as I came out from identifying his body—there were no injuries visible to me—I could not cease imagining Robert's arms aching to enfold me again as they had with such astonishing confidence in 1977.

I did not wait until Christmas but wrote the day after the funeral:

> *Dear Robert,*
> *Stephen died in a car crash driving back from his parents'.*

I realise now that I'd never told him I had a partner.

I've lots of people to write to, but first things first.

Clever sentence that, both ranking Robert among the lots and giving him a special status. He can take it how he likes.

But having told you I hardly know what else to say. It will be hard to think of myself as a single man again. Perhaps you never do become single again after a deep experience of connection, no matter how long. Or short.

Through the ether I will him to understand that.

Yet already—and don't think this is callous, it isn't—I'm reaching out towards the idea of a new relationship. Mark.

There was no reply until Christmas, and then there was nothing at all written in the card, just a typewritten slip: "Tough about you and Simon. David & Robert."

I winced. I'd caused little rat-faced David suddenly to assert himself in that grand balconied flat high up in Kelvin Court: "Just an old friend, you say. Christ, he's practically begging you to go and live with him. No, *I'll* see to the card. I'm going to put a stop to this."

In 1991 there was nothing from them, nor in 1992. Robert had decided that I must be sacrificed to protect his relationship with David. I should never hear from him again. I admired his honesty, for it would have been easy to send me a card on the sly with an injunction not to mention it in mine. I did what Robert wanted and stopped sending to him.

And several years passed in silence. Indeed, I moved away from Glasgow, got a job in Croydon. But not before, on a passing inspiration, I'd gone into the local public library and asked for the register of electors and looked up Kelvin Court. I liked seeing Robert's name in a list with everyone else's. Here he was, rubbing shoulders with all and sundry. He had indeed moved on, as people do in cities.

But the trophy I sought and acquired as I sat at the table with old men reading newspapers, the trophy I'd failed to capture that night outside Kelvin Court, was David's surname: Duffy. It was something I possessed in secret, like pornography at the bottom of a drawer. "You don't know I know David's surname," I would think, down in Croydon, my defiant little thought winging up to Glasgow.

And next Christmas I got a card, forwarded by the people who had bought my flat, and with it was one of those dreadful printed newsletters to the world that say: behold us and admire. It had to be David's idea; certainly, my salt-of-the-earth Robert could never have come up with such poncy self-satisfied words. They had had a "very successful" holiday in Goa. They had two dogs, Ginger and Posh, "which we sometimes mistake for the children which, we have been told by the doctors, we can never have." Ho, ho, ho. The unspoken message to me was: we are so bloody secure now that we can treat you to a little patronising notice.

Robert's bombshell arrived three weeks ago:

You have to know David and I have split up. He wants children and is looking for a woman to give him kids. Its a farce, she wo'nt give him anything else he wants, thats for sure, heh heh.

"Heh heh." Hardly the words of someone whose life

has just been shattered. Oh, but a boy like, someone like, Robert just doesn't have the vocabulary to express what's going on in his fond loving core.

So here I am, stepping off the 'plane, beginning the trudge along the tedious airport corridors that will lead me to—what?

I sent him a postcard saying, "Arriving Glasgow airport 10-15 Friday night, British Midland flight from Heathrow. Meet?" The last word could be passed off merely as a suggestion that we might meet for a chat during a stay in Glasgow made for other reasons.

And here is the desk, deserted at this time of night, where the corridors emerge into the public area, and my eye surveys the people waiting for arrivals. They look so drab and spiritless you can hardly credit them with real feelings.

Among them is a man in a brown suede carcoat with velvet collar. He looks down, smiling secretly to himself. Yes, he has gone bald, almost entirely so, and the hair that's left straggles over the collar. He's not tried to keep middle-age at bay by shaving it close.

Ah, but once you have fancied someone, why, the person you have fancied is always invisibly there.

We shake hands like people meeting for the first time, though our fingers have so often exchanged touch through Christmas cards. I do not know what to say.

I say, "So what was the business?"

I mean, what sort of business, but he thinks I am asking for the name and says, "Music Markdown." Surprisingly, I know of it: cut-price CDs by mail-order, run from an address on the south side. Actually, I used to buy CDs from the firm. In fact, lots. (Correction: Stephen and I did.) So the post had woven further threads between us, invisible to me. The order-form in my handwriting had gone from our hall table to Robert's dusty office, not that he would have recognised my name. (Did the form say, in small print at the top, "Proprietor: R. McHugh"? I try to call it up in my memory and look.)

He repeats his firm's name, dividing the second word into two, and I feel a great jolt of joy before I realise why I feel it.

He is saying: "You have to know. I was very happy with David. Until."

And I have to say, "So was I with Stephen." But these are mere diplomatic formalities, for I see my name in neon on an industrial unit, a wee warehouse, radiating out into the Glasgow night like a star calling the Magi to make a journey.

The authority at the core of him carries us in silence to the airport exit, but it is the blessed silence of people who have nothing that needs discussing. And after all, we have a long history of silence between us.

As we cross the road to the car-park all the airport lights create an unreal science-fiction landscape that has nothing to do with homely things like, oh, hair over a collar and Christmas cards and bell-pushes. The illuminated sign on Robert's warehouse zooms upwards in the night, growing and growing until it dwarfs the city, until the whole of Glasgow is nothing but the huddled base and support for a tower of masts and props and pylons miles high which rotates a vast flashing sign, "Mark Down". It shines year in, year out, though the city's life goes on as it always does.

AN EPISODE OF
RURAL DEPOPULATION

The trouble began where Glen Buchan meets the outside world, where the hilly arms that embrace it descend and curve round and almost touch. That was a long way from Jack and me, for our house stands at the head of the glen. It is a castle, actually, a sixteenth-century tower-house that we have lovingly restored. I like to think that cementing the stones has cemented us, too.

The castle has no entry at ground level. The door is high in the unharled wall and was originally reached only by a ladder that was pulled up. This was for defensive purposes. It made me anxious when the authorities made us build a staircase up to the door. Someone might get in.

I shall not describe Jack. He plays no part in this story. He is simply the person you love, if any. Anyway, I know no more about him than you do, setting aside irrelevant things like what he looks like naked and habits of the leaving-the-toothpaste-cap-off kind.

Our tower, from which we often fly a flag bearing our entwined initials, stands on the crown of a hill. To north and south of us the hill throws out eastward-running ridges enclosing a strath of unknown farmlands, and each ridge is graced by three special homes which, together with our tower, are known as the Higher Houses. I liked to think that this was because they were inhabited by brave and loving couples. It was nice to know they were there, the other couples. Their inevitable happiness sustained

Jack and me. By some trick of the Aberdeenshire light we could see clearly each of the other Higher Houses and its distant couple, even the ones far away towards the glen mouth. Boldly, Jack and I would wave to them from our tower, and when they waved back from balcony or terrace or dormer window we would feel blessed, as though immortals were conferring immortality.

Down below, the pattern of the fields, with little farmhouses placed among them like promises, had a beauty that I liked to think was nature's sympathetic reflection of the love that made couples of all us couples. This beauty could sometimes make you feel there was nothing to dread.

As I said, the trouble entered at the glen mouth. In the old stone Gate House to the estate lived what looked the ideal young couple (IYC) you see in photographs in an estate agent's window. He was still boyish, but his chin and buttocks assured you he was ready for a man's responsibility. She was golden-haired and eager, absolutely free from any idea of there being a role for a woman to fill. Through windows you would glimpse them sanding floors, plastering. They would be seen to pause in their labours and open champagne, sitting cross-legged amid the loving disorder, toasting each other and the brightness of an IYC's future, exchanging kisses, eyes shining, charmingly barefoot.

Across the glen mouth Buchan House, once the laird's house, was grand enough to have been run for a time as a 'country house hotel'. White-haired Amabel Fyfe, our nearest Higher House neighbour, had worked there. "You would not believe the adultery," she would cry, but I would.

"Writing down different surnames with their wedding

rings still on!" she would say in a rising shout.

"They could be widows and widowers," I would say, a spell to ward off evil, or, "Today lots of wives keep their own names."

Still, I was glad when the hotel failed. Buchan House became the home of the Loadsas, as we called them after they left. He had made money in transport during the oil boom, and his burly body still looked cramped from the cab of a lorry. His face was mean-looking, but actually he wasn't mean, for he carried banknotes in fat rolls and gave them away freely. A farmchild, shyly asking to be backed in a sponsored silence to raise money for computers at the school to which she was bussed daily, couldn't believe his putting down for £250 an hour. When we feared that the nearest shop and post-office, which was in a village seven miles away, was going to shut, he bought it and kept it going—at a huge loss, so Amabel reported. And when the IYC needed stone to add a proper bathroom onto the Gate House, he got it for them cheap.

Thin Mrs Loadsa always seemed dressed for the directors' table at the company dinner-dance. Her elaborate hairstyles and extremely high-heeled shoes did not last long in the winds and rain and mud of the glen. When standing next to her husband she tended to look away.

Mr Loadsa took to going across to the Gate House about the stone, and then one day he and the female half of the IYC were seen kissing behind the pile of it. Afterwards you noticed when you peeped in that the renovations were no further advanced and no-one lived there. Amabel reported that the male half was living with his parents in Ellon.

"No idea of their duty, these young ones," Amabel

cried. "It's happiness they're after."

"Happiness!" My doctor had pronounced the C-word.

I stammered, "It's all right, they couldn't *really* have loved each other, for they weren't married." The lump's probably just a, you know, swollen gland…

Soon Buchan House fell empty, too. "Divorced him!" Amabel cried in a voice that, had God been sitting on the clouds above Glen Buchan, would have left Him in no doubt just how wicked divorces are. I made the best I could of the divorce. Some people said the thing with the female half of the IYC was the last straw after a long stream of infidelities (a girl in every truck stop), but I liked to think it was his only lapse and Mrs Loadsa divorced Mr because she was a dedicated soldier in the same cause as Jack and I, or at least I, waging total war against the enemy, even at the cost of her own happiness. Her persistence with her high heels and elaborate hair styles in the face of the glen weather had been of a piece with this.

I took comfort, too, in Darby and Joan, i.e. Roddy and Amabel. With her headscarf and long skirts and crisp white apron and clog-like shoes, Amabel looked like a dancing old peasant woman in a Breughel painting, though of course without the air of being ready for debauchery. Despite belonging to the aristocracy of the heart Amabel actually was a peasant, she and Roddy having risen from the farmlands below. They'd spent all their savings on having a large prefabricated bungalow built on the southern ridge, getting it past the planning authorities as repair of an old shieling. They were just down the shoulder from me and Jack, and their proximity made me feel safe, as if we lived next door to a police-station. Roddy, white-haired like her, had a flat weather-reddened face still redder from bashfulness. When he spoke, which was not often, you expected the mystic deliverances of Highland second sight but what you heard, in a hurried yelp, was that he had had a nice egg for breakfast, something like that. Their fifty years of married life were a healthy counterweight to the Loadsa divorce.

True, without Mr Loadsa's money the shop and post-office shut down, and the nearest was now thirteen miles away, but that was the necessary price, like slaughtering badgers to prevent bovine TB.

Not that it eliminated the contagion. The next to succumb were the two Roberts, Rob and Bob. This gay couple inhabited the Old Kirk, which had been converted into an open-plan home with areas for sitting and cooking and dining and sleeping. Through a lancet window you looked straight onto their very large bed. Each had curly black hair and the soft confiding face of a creature made to be kept as a pet. You would see them dawdling together on the hillsides, shirtless in fine weather, giving each other shy smiles but speaking rarely, as if speech were needless for happiness. Both worked in an advertising agency in Aberdeen and somehow did not look quite right in their suits as you saw them driving off in the morning side by side in their BMW.

There came the day when Rob banged on our door and as I let him into the kitchen, snug despite the raw stone walls, his lips pulled themselves back into an uncontrollable grimace. I stared at his teeth, so abandoned and vulnerable. Through sobs he wailed, "Bob is screwing around."

Even more alarmingly, Bob had done it right under Rob's nose, trips out of the office 'to see a client' being in fact visits to the Marine Club Sauna, Aberdeen.

Jack was out somewhere.

"I won't put up with it. He says it's just sex, but sex is never just sex. Bob and I are finished."

"Quite right," I said.

"I'll burn the fucking place down."

I said, "You do that."

I said, "How did you find out?"

"I met him in there." He burst into new tears that invited a consoling arm around his shoulders.

There was a sudden rapping on the door. I prayed it was Bob, Bob pursuing, Bob repentant, Bob with miraculous power to expunge what had happened from history and reinstate their exemplary, idyllic life together.

But it was Amabel breathless, Amabel vigorous. "He's fallen," she yelled, and we all, Rob and I and old Amabel, sprinted down the shoulder of the hill to where Roddy had fallen from a ladder while cleaning gutters. Our good-hearted unanimity of concern for Roddy was such a restorative after Rob's depressing news.

And so was Amabel's behaviour afterwards. Roddy had to go permanently into a care home at Banff where medical attention was always at hand. But three times a week Amabel walked the six-mile length of the glen to get the thrice-weekly bus past the glen mouth that would take her to visit him, and then in the evening walked the six miles back up the glen. "Wife's duty," she barked. More than ever, Amabel and Roddy became our beacon. In her dear familiar eyes I liked to detect the devotion and greatness of heart that come when you're old.

And besides her visiting regime, arduous enough for a woman in her seventies, Amabel kept up her housekeeping job at the Shooting Lodge, for she needed the money.

The Shooting Lodge was surplus to requirements now that the wealthy foreign shooters were transported in from city hotels by fast cars. Of the couple who bought it, you saw Hugh at windows, staring out, bulky and untidy but always with a bow-tie, which allowed you to think he was basically cheerful about things. He was said to be preoccupied with the Picts. It was Marianne, as plump and placid as a successful marriage, her hair in burnished braids around her head, who impressed herself upon you. All alone in her quilted jacket, she walked the footpaths she knew so well as though exploring them. Her serene smile was a descent of grace, an authoritative assurance that you and the life you lived were admirable. During her long periods away, Amabel strode back and forth along the ridge to housekeep for poor Hugh.

No-one gave any thought to Marianne's absences until during one of them Hugh descended off the balcony of the Shooting Lodge and smashed his head and died.

"Not an accident," said Amabel.

"Oh, but you said he drank, all the empties you had to take out, that was the inquest verdict, Accident, we mustn't doubt the public authorities."

"He gave her warning," she cried from the ridge above the innocent beauty of fields and farms, "that he would throw himself to his death the very next time she went away to—"

"An elderly relation, I've always thought."

"—her lover!" With pride and scorn Amabel bawled the completion of her sentence to the winds. "That is what she called it."

After the long drive from the crematorium the remaining inhabitants of the Higher Houses gathered at the Shooting Lodge. Funerals should bring consolation and, yes, I could feel Hugh had done me a service, for (a) he could be seen as a hero of passive resistance, a Buddhist monk burning himself to death while the occupying forces strut in triumphal procession, yet (b) his throwing himself from his balcony somehow pre-empted my throwing myself from our tower, should Jack ever leave me. By now we all knew that Marianne, quietly moving among us with sherry, had told Hugh on their marriage that she would spend half the year with a man who ran salmon farms near Oban. From the blinked-away tears and her quiet broken references to her irreparable loss, you would have thought you were looking on grief incarnate—a valuable lesson in how the Devil disguises himself. I said pointedly, "Has anyone else noticed through the lancet window that the Old Kirk floor has rotted and collapsed since the place was abandoned? Divine judgement on *open-plan living*."

Professor Lickleyhead murmured, "It's sound evolutionary strategy for a woman to have two mates. More variation in the offspring, more support for the offspring, therefore more chance of the offspring surviving and therefore of her genes surviving."

So nature, too, was engaged in the conspiracy to undermine the most precious thing in the world or out of it. I looked through the French windows at the heather just coming into bloom, and knew that this year it would not strike me, as it usually strikes people, as more purple than ever before.

"But she hasn't got any children," was the best protest I could manage, too loudly because Marianne turned and gave me one of her enhancing smiles.

Professor Lickleyhead, who had dashing sideburns, lived in the Old Manse. His wife, a pretty little woman, had been his secretary and still was, in a way. He was bony and tall, and his trousers were never long enough. You would see him putting rubbish into the bin furtively, as though this were not to be counted as part of the life of Professor Lickleyhead.

He and I had strolled out through the French windows to a little stone seat in a shelter that had a canopy of antlers. He sat down and patted the seat for me to join him, and when I did, the hand that had patted the seat squeezed my crotch.

I said, "Is this sound evolutionary strategy, too?"

His eyes surveyed next year's research budget or the audience at a learned conference. "There is a good deal of support for the kin-selection hypothesis, according to which that part of the population with a disposition towards sexual acts with those of the same gender tends to contribute resources to the offspring of its siblings, with whom, of course, it shares genes, therefore facilitating the survival of its own genes." My question must have reached him as consent, for as he spoke he squeezed and stroked more systematically.

"But this is infidelity. It's not right."

"*Infidelity? Right?*" I was Jane Goodall, perversely attributing feelings to chimpanzees (not, alas, monogamous) instead of confining her scientific reports to their overt behaviour.

"It's only gay," he snapped, his face wearing its taking-out-the-rubbish look, as I ran indoors for refuge with Jack. Over the glen mouth dark clouds rolled in like a long-fated invasion, and great gusts splattered raindrops. Jack and I began the drive back to our tower through a howling maelstrom that made the whole glen a place of horror and desolation.

But nature had its poetic revenge on one who had conscripted it to undermine love. I learned the next day that the storm blew down an ancient Scots pine onto the

Old Manse, causing masonry to kill Professor Lickleyhead as he lay in his bed. When Amabel told me that his wife, whom we saw no more (for she had no-one in the glen to be secretary to), survived because they slept in separate rooms, I was warmed by an even stronger sense of an upholding plan.

And so were left, in the Higher Houses, just Jack and I plus Amabel, who still visited her Roddy thrice-weekly and sometimes had him delivered home by ambulance for weekends. In some ways these were not bad years. (1) Jack and I were no longer surrounded by couples whose richness of connection made us feel as though a secret was being withheld from us. (2) Hugh's death (I'd been sure before that it had done me a service!) activated a secret self-healing mechanism that disinfected Glen Buchan by causing Marianne to move to Florida. She fled her husband's ashes, which, from below, we had watched her scatter into the rhododendrons from his fatal balcony, a queen dispensing favours; she also abandoned the salmon-farmer, whom I liked to think of as suffering all the horrible pangs I'd suffer if Jack left me, for he had been complicit in adultery. (3) Amabel's continuing devotion to Roddy was a continuing inspiration. (4) There was cheering news in the *Press and Journal* that the Marine Club had burned down. The report of Rob's trial stated that he smuggled in paraffin, just another person carrying a plastic mineral-water bottle. The bodies of six naked men were found in the ruins. All these signs encouraged confidence that our love would survive.

Then on one of his weekend visits home Roddy crawled the mile along the ridge to our castle and yelped up our stone staircase that Amabel was dead.

She wasn't, but she'd had a stroke. Roddy was whisked

back to his care home and a social worker, who was young and sweet-faced and called people by their Christian names, came to arrange for Amabel to follow. Amabel's speech, because of the stroke, was incomprehensible to her, so I interpreted.

"Gurgh uum ae yooyeem gurgh shyash toep netterth eearghy."

"So long as I can be with him, that's all that matters to me."

If I reported that as what she'd intended to bark, who would be the wiser?

Amabel, yes, but she had no mouthpiece but me.

Her eyes were just orbs with colour and mobility.

The social worker's voice tinkled, "Did you catch what Amabel said, Terrance?"

I stared at the lurid orange and yellow sworls of Amabel's carpet and heard myself say, "What *Mrs Fyfe* said, *Ms Puttock*, is, 'I've done my duty to him. Send me to Perth, I've my sister lives there.' "

Why, oh why, did I say it? In a rush of self-justification I allowed mad maxims like *Honesty is the best policy* and *The truth shall make you free* to rattle in my mind, but actually I was an ecological criminal. I'd made a vast hole in the ozone layer that protects Glen Buchan.

Amabel nodded with her old vigour and was put down for a care home near Perth, 100 miles from her Roddy. I comforted my guilty conscience by reflecting that she might have been able to contradict me by writing down her evil wish.

As I saw the sweet-faced social worker out her sing-song voice delivered the final blow: "It's a valid choice, Terrance, that female clients do often choose as regards the care accommodation options as regards themselves and their husbands."

So the evidence is against us, Jack and me. From our castle at the head of the glen we look out upon the ruins of the other Higher Houses, and I struggle to realise that Jack is actually holding my hand. I recall the couples we once waved to, and I shiver at the huge disfiguring stripes spreading on the hills in a variety of greens, as if they are the visible manifestation of foot and mouth disease encircling an uninfected enclave that must inevitably succumb, though I know they are only caused by controlled burnings, in different years, for the sake of the game birds. The farmlands below are no longer in their beauty an outward expression of our love but a glimpse of another world, perfect, unattainable, where unknown people are happy. But we do our best, Jack and I: we ignore the evidence, as we have done for thirty years, and we fly our brave flag with our initials entwined.

THE TWELVE DAYS
OF CHRISTMAS

Nothing matters in itself, only the experiences you have of it. And I had all the experiences of love in twelve days, leaving me free to get on with my life.

DECEMBER 24TH: LOVE AT FIRST SIGHT

It was just as it's supposed to be: some enchanted evening, a stranger, eyes across a crowded room. It took place up at Jerry Mahony's on Christmas Eve, a last chance for the guys to be themselves before going home to their families for Christmas. He was among the crowd dancing to Diana Ross, 1970s thin with shaggy springy black hair and John Lennon glasses. His arms jerked like a marionette's pulled from the wrists, his open mouth and closed eyes mimicked a trance. Just as I'd worked out he was dancing by himself, he opened his eyes and reconfigured the world, the universe, around me. I thought he'd mistaken me for someone, but next thing he'd pushed through the crowd and was standing before me, smiling, saying nothing, blithe like a child who trusts the genie to grant his wish.

If you go to a watchnight service on Christmas Eve you can get the feeling of some great world-transforming event coming about: how silently, how silently, the wondrous gift is given. We felt that, Conrad and I. Love came down at Christmas.

DECEMBER 25TH: A NEW WORLD

The world-transformed feeling wasn't temporary. It lasted all Christmas Day. We woke in my bed, full of wonder. As I pulled back the curtains and looked at the stone facade of the flats opposite, it was good, this year, to imagine the people unwrapping presents, preparing turkeys, etcetera.

He called from the bed, "You'll get arrested for indecent exposure."

"I'll put tinsel round my penis, that'll make it okay." Somehow I couldn't use a less clinical word. Shivering, I jumped back into bed and his embrace.

I tried out irony: "Sorry I didn't get you a Christmas present."

"Mikey"—I'd always been strictly *Michael*, yet here I was with a lover's pet-name for me!—"the best present I could ever have is you." His voice ached with the pressure of sincerity, and the giggle that followed in no way undercut what he'd said.

The turkey breast I'd got for myself would do for two but we decided to try to find a shop open and buy a Christmas pudding. In the deserted streets I kept stopping to look at familiar Glasgow tenements, because they seemed rebuilt in a new world. An Indian shopkeeper wished us Merry Christmas handing over a pudding. I took a risk and said, "We're in love," and he smiled as though blessing us, but his English wasn't too good and perhaps he only thought I'd said one of the rote Christmas phrases.

Outside, Conrad said, "Stay there, Mikey," and popped back in.

"For servant-boy's honourable celestial much-beloved Mikey." He had bowed low in a vaguely oriental manner, his outstretched hands making a salver to present a bubble-blowing kit. As dusk descended on that cold damp Christmas afternoon and we glimpsed Christmas dinners through lighted windows, we blew soap bubbles all the way back to my flat.

Everyone's love has to contain a memory like that.

DECEMBER 26TH: OUR FIRST QUARREL

"Hey," I said, "Let's go to the pantomime. The perfect thing for Boxing Day. *Babes in the Wood.*" I was already looking up the box-office number.

He said, "Nah," and I said, "Transformation scenes and *Look out behind you!* and join-in songs. We'll be kids together, *we'll* be the babes in the wood."

"You can go."

I stopped dialling. "Not by myself. Why can't you tune in to this?"

"Mikey, listen. *I don't want to go to a pantomime.*"

I had no idea who this was. Human shape deceived you, other people were insuperably alien. Love didn't exist anywhere.

But I remembered about communicating and negotiating, etcetera, and although there was no longer anything that I wanted to achieve by them, I said obediently, "Is there anywhere *you* would like to go?"

"The La Scala has a James Bond double-bill."

"You actually *like* Bond films?" I washed the despair from my voice, forced eagerness into it, consciously opened up bright vistas. "Hey, yes, not Christmassy at all, that could be fun."

Growing, is what they call it; growing together. Getting outside the shell of your selfishness, entering into your lover's tastes and viewpoint. Been there, done that.

DECEMBER 27TH:
SETTLING DOWN AFTER THE HONEYMOON

For the first couple of days we couldn't get enough sex: before we slept, in the night, waking in the morning, during the day. In the back row of the movies yesterday we were the teenagers we'd not been allowed to be. He unzipped me, I pulled out his shirt at the back and stroked the vulnerable line where skin supplanted the leather of his belt. Afterwards we didn't say a word, we just stopped a taxi—I can't remember which of us did it, we'd become one mind, one person—and all the way home he looked at me in silence as if he hurt with delight in me, and we ran, literally ran, up the stairs of the close and were pulling each other's clothes off before I'd pushed the door shut behind us in my little windowless hallway.

But now things were cooling down. Waking this morning we didn't have sex.

"That's fine," I said. "The old country saying: put a bean in a jar every time you have sex the first year you're married, take one out every time after that, and you'll never empty the jar."

To which he made the response, "In a real relationship like ours sex isn't the only thing, there's so much else."

Actually to be in a position where we could say such things!

DECEMBER 28TH: FAMILY HOSTILITY

We had the family hostility bit, too, like Romeo and Juliet.

I'd not even 'phoned my parents over Christmas, they having made their views about me all too clear, but Conrad's love made me strong.

When she heard my voice my mother said, "Michael!

So you got through despite the strikes." Weird but it showed willing about letting bygones.

"I've got news. I've fallen in love."

She was delighted. "Well! When are we going to meet her?"

"Not her. Him."

Silence. Then in a bright voice suitable to spiffing news: "Janet and Brian and the children are staying till New Year."

"Great. We'll come over. My nephews can meet their new uncle."

"Christmas isn't the time for arguments." Her more-in-sorrow voice. "Let's all just try and be happy together."

"And who's *all*? Does *all* include Conrad? Because let me tell you, Conrad is the biggest thing that's ever happened to me, and I try to share it with my family and...."

I looked at Conrad, politely looking at a magazine. His lips, considered in isolation, were too defined, too pointed at the ends.

I completed, "...And my bloody mother kicks me in the teeth!" I remembered to slam down the 'phone.

I was trembling, gasping, and Conrad's arms were around me. "Mikey, Mikey. But you've got new family now: me. You and me alone against the world, loving each other the deeper for that."

DECEMBER 29TH: INFIDELITY

When he came back to my flat on Christmas Eve he only had the clothes he stood up in. No problem, he could wear mine, which straight couples can't do unless they're kinky. I liked to watch him putting on a shirt of mine, underpants that were mine.

But then he said he needed to go and fetch things.

I said, "I'll come with you. I want to see your flat—your world—"

He stopped my mouth with a kiss. "Nah. It'll just be, you know, a flying visit."

The tea was spoiling by the time he got back. And he didn't have much luggage, just some clothes in a couple of Templeton's supermarket bags. And instead of embracing me after several hours' absence, he turned away.

"On the way I picked someone up in Kelvingrove Park and took them back to my flat." Rapid, toneless.

I couldn't remember the script.

"You shit! After I burnt my bridges with my parents for you."

No, that wouldn't be the right reply. The mature reply.

I said, "That's just physical release, absolutely nothing to do with what we've got between us."

I stopped his mouth with a kiss, though I could not help thinking of where the mouth might have been so very recently.

So I know what it is to forgive an unfaithful lover and enlarge your love beyond the cosy lovey-dovey kind.

DECEMBER 30TH: COMMITMENT

After we'd made love this morning he said, "I'm going back to sleep. I can't sleep properly, two in a single bed."

"But we have breakfast together. I like passing you the marmalade and things."

"Mikey, that won't get me through the day when I have to go to work. I'll need sleep."

He asleep in his flat, me in my bed here. Our home broken up.

I curled away.

No connection between us was possible, of any kind.

He kissed the back of my neck. "The sales are on. Let's go out and buy a double bed."

It was the beginning of the world again, and glory shone around.

In the gloomy discount warehouse smelling of paraffin heaters, a redundant church, we sat side by side on beds, testing them. I said with naughty loudness, "We need to make sure the springs are strong enough to stand lot of bouncing up and down," and was rewarded with a glare from a passing stately fat woman. Her tartan-trimmed green coat was poised open to show a jumper of the exact-same green and a tartan skirt matching the trim. Lipstick, gloves, glasses were the same orangey-red as her hair.

Under her disapproval Conrad put a defiant arm around my shoulders. My protector.

I pronounced, "Bridegrooms always feel panic at the altar. Yesterday was merely the last gasp of uncertainty before commitment."

We each wrote a cheque for half the amount, challenging the assistant to make difficulties. Just the naming of the delivery date, in the second week of January, seemed to guarantee our commitment to each other.

DECEMBER 31ST: OUR ANNIVERSARY

Anniversaries: times to look back and take stock.

On Hogmanay I said, "Only a week, but we've lived a whole lifetime. Everything before Christmas is B.C. Before Conrad."

He said, "I never thought I was cut out for a relationship till there was you."

All our lives we'd been secretly rehearsing for the day we could say things like that.

I said, "Jerry Mahony's tonight will be a bore. Yattering to other people when I only want to be with you."

"Mikey, let's have New Year in a world of our own."

A magical idea.

We got the most expensive whisky in Haddows. We had *television* on for the bells, and those relentless party faces bawling out *Happy New Year* seemed so inane and false.

We toasted our love, we kissed gently, we kissed passionately, I turned off the television, we made love. We were big enough, the pair of us, to carry the burden and hope of the new year all by ourselves.

JANUARY 1ST: PUBLIC RECOGNITION

I was being chatted up, no doubt about it.

He was an odd little guy with a turned-up face wrinkled like an old man's. People called him The Pixie and said he'd been a boxer. He was saying, "Opportunity doesn't come twice, life is short, you've got to take your chance, seize the moment." He had tried this patter on everyone.

Just the quiet way Conrad arrived with my drink told him everything. He looked from Conrad to me and back. "Sorry, didn't realise."

I gave him a nice smile.

Apart from little Arnie Pixie everyone else up at Jerry Mahony's on New Year's Day seemed to know. Jerry himself paid us a huge tribute. I need to explain that despite keeping open house for the guys, or perhaps because of it, Jerry was a tremendous cynic about love and relationships. For example: when Torquil got off with Cliff he put on *Will You Still Love Me Tomorrow?* as they left, and later he'd refer to them as Tartsky and Clutch. But talking to you he made you feel you were exempt from this attitude and he looked up to you as a standard-bearer of true love. It was behind people's backs that he said the cynical things. Well, look what he said in the kitchen about us when he didn't know I overheard: "Conrad and Michael are the nicest thing that's happened for a long time. There's hope for us all."

We made a point of dancing to *You Are Everything*, and people fell back to give us privileged space. When we moved into each other's arms and slow-danced beneath the wonderful plaster rose in Jerry Mahony's eighteen-foot ceiling, Conrad's hard-on pressed against me, there was a sound like a collective sigh and I heard *Conrad'n'Michael* whispered like a single name.

JANUARY 2ND: JUST AN ORDINARY DAY

There are songs about an uneventful day magically transformed because the two people doing ordinary things are in love. *Manhattan*. Lou Reed's *Perfect Day*.

This was a day like that. We sat around, we did a washing (mixing our clothes in the machine!), we watched television, we went out for the stuff for him to make his curry. It was as if the unassigned secret days of Christmas and New Year would go on for ever. Nothing to tell, and yet bliss.

No, one thing to tell. I'd started to say something and the doorbell went. It was old Mrs Veitch from downstairs saying she had a burst pipe and the water was being turned off for a bit. Afterwards I said to Conrad, "I can't remember what I was going to tell you," and he said, "Don't fuss about it, Mikey."

But then he said: "We've got the rest of our lives to tell each other things."

JANUARY 3RD: IT'S OVER

But that was a golden day before the end. Holidays were finished, the world re-opened for business, its imperatives dragged people out of the tunnel of private days. He 'phoned me at my work from his work.

"Mikey, I'm not coming back."

"Staying at your flat tonight." But I knew.

"I'm not coming back at all."

"Right." You pretend there's nothing needs explaining. "What about your stuff?"

"I'll get it tomorrow when you're not there."

"That's best. Put your key through the letter-box after. What about the joint property?"

"Mikey, don't fuss. You don't owe me anything. The past doesn't exist. I bought that bed for your house because it was how I felt at the time."

I was ready with what came next. "We'll stay friends."

"Always, Mikey."

So I've had the cool civilized parting.

JANUARY 4TH:
"I CAN'T LIVE WITHOUT YOU."

I've had the other kind, too.

He began it with a really dramatic surprise. I got home from work this evening to a forsaken flat, I switched on the light in the main room, and there he was on my settee with his two Templeton's plastic bags at his feet.

"I tried to leave three hours ago, but it's no good. I can't live without you."

Hands up everyone who's actually had that said to them!

He stood. My cue. My arms went around him. I narrated: "Last night I buried my face in one of your plastic bags just to smell you for the last time."

"Mikey!" Ridicule, but loving ridicule that promised to assuage all my pain forever.

It was the best sex we ever had.

"Because," I said, showing that I, too, could reconfigure the world, abolish the past, "now we really know how much we mean to each other."

I was watching him button on his shirt. He turned away. "It's no good, Mikey."

He said, "It's all so perfect, we'd only go downhill."

He said, "We've given all we had to give. I'd rather leave while I'm in love."

My turn. I mused, "It's like that song. We've just had sex to say goodbye. Make believe you love me one more time."

He wailed, "I love you, Mikey." Each hand took up a plastic bag, he stood there like someone about to be dragged off to prison. It was the opportunity for me to do the noble thing, comfort him for leaving me. I said, "Don't worry about me. I'll get along." We kissed tenderly.

"Hey, Mikey, we're mingling our tears!" He was radiant that we'd done that.

I made myself watch him all the way down the close stairs with his plastic bags and, like the end of a film, he never looked back.

Not then. But I passed him in the street today, and he did look back.

"Mikey!" My pet-name after all the years; decades, actually.

His hair is silver-grey now but his granny glasses are just the same. So was his attention, so complete that the universe was recreated around me.

"We had good times, Mikey. We *were* the babes in the

wood."

He said, "Hey, that amazing red and green woman."

He said, "Hey, The Pixie's a member of parliament now, in the Scottish Parliament."

I ventured, "The bubble pipe?"

"It was a wire blower you dipped in."

"Ah yes, I remember it well."

By the time he was saying, with his giggle-gurgle of delight, "Have you ever worn tinsel around your clinical term?" I was feeling stunned by joy and by what the joy told me. If experiences remain alive—in both of you, too—what does it matter that the events have disappeared into time and the person is walking on, saying "Speak to you soon" in the way people say it when they won't? I haven't missed out. I've had a love of my own.

HIS STEADFAST LOVE

He flipped open the book at random. I caused it to open so that these words caught his eye: "His steadfast love endures for ever."

He has gasped audibly. At this moment he is nothing but an ache of yearning. And that yearning is too big to be satisfied anywhere except in me. I've hooked him!

I freeze the frame for a moment to enjoy my success. I wouldn't ask others to be fishers of men if I were not pretty good at it myself.

Half an hour ago, going by time, I watched him slam the door and make that clatter going downstairs that sounds like defiance and purpose. In fact, he was driven out by nothing but the intolerableness of his pain. Silly boy, to have got himself into the position where he was vulnerable to so much suffering.

It blew up out of nothing, this row, this breach, this (as I firmly intend it to be) ending. As rows and breaches and endings so often do. The transcript makes awfully banal reading.

*ALEX is ensconced in an armchair reading **The Guardian**. At the table JAMIE is sorting papers, bills, letters. His glances at Alex resemble those of someone who hesitates to disturb him.*

JAMIE:
This invitation from Robert—I told him we'd go.

ALEX:
Well, you can go.

JAMIE:

Oh. But I accepted for us both.

ALEX:

[*smiling, relaxed, warm, no hint of sharpness*]
Easily remedied!

JAMIE:

But, but you didn't tell me you didn't want to go. When I told you about Robert's invitation.

ALEX:

[*still smiling*]

Well, I'm telling you now.

JAMIE:

[*with incredulity on the third word*]
But why not?

ALEX:

[*musingly, as though it were merely an interesting problem*]
I don't know.

JAMIE:

But it'll look odd, me without you.

Alex widens his smile and his eyes, inviting Jamie to think what a silly thing he's just said.

JAMIE:

I suppose I could say you've got a migraine.

ALEX:

Good old **my**graine. Or **mee**graine.

JAMIE:

[*with irritation*]

Well, what else can I say?

ALEX:

[*in the patient voice with which you tell a child in a
tantrum of impatience that the way to build the model
airplane is to take one step at a time*]

Now why do you have to say anything? You can just
report, quite truthfully, that I wasn't in the mood for a
party.

JAMIE:

[*after a wounded silence*]

What's this about? Really?

ALEX:

It's not about anything. I just don't want to go to Robert's
fucking party.

JAMIE:

It's not a fucking party. Robert's too prim to throw that
sort of party.

For a moment they smiled together, quite genuinely, at
the wit, such as it was. They have always enjoyed verbal
plays. It's one of their foundations. You, reader, are
incredulous: "Something as flimsy as that—a *foundation*?
For love, lifelong union, etc?" But anything at all can be a
foundation; I know. If they could have rested on that little

foundation—if Alex had replied, with a wee genuflexion towards the jealous possessiveness that Jamie craves to find in him, "Ah well, I can let you go without worrying, then"—all would have been well. From their point of view, that is, though not from mine, for I am in the business of bringing a sword between a man and those of his own household. But they missed their chance, and instead...

ALEX:
If you choose to go, Jamie, you'll have to steel yourself to get by without parading as one half of a couple.

JAMIE:
Oh, I'm used to that. I get a lot of practice in not feeling half of a couple.

ALEX:
[*very considerately*]
I can tell how much that disappoints you. Maybe it's time to cut your losses, then.

JAMIE:
Do you mean what I think you mean?

ALEX:
[*with complete amiability*]
What do you think I mean?

JAMIE:
Are you proposing to dump me? Is that clear enough for you? After twenty years?

ALEX:

[*dispassionately, like a good liberal whose opinions are never fixed in stone*]

Perhaps it is something that should be talked through. Considered.

JAMIE:

[*eyes bulging*]

In my book there's no difference between "I'm thinking of dumping you" and "I hereby dump you." If you can even for one moment even think of dumping me, then you have already abandoned the enduring permanent absolute commitment that I thought we had. You simply don't love me. Not with the enduring permanent absolute love that, that, that, that I love you with.

Jamie puts on shoes and jacket as quickly as possible, in parentheses to minimise the indignity of these operations. He stamps out, slamming the door.

Those of you who claim to know about relationships will say, "A relationship as long as that couldn't have ended over something as trivial as a party invitation. There must have been a lot of big unresolved problems that weren't talked about and dealt with." Well, I, who spy everything with my little eye, know otherwise. That, my dears, is exactly how cookies and relationships do crumble. Big Unresolved Problems?—Away and look for the Loch Ness Monster.

Down the road went Jamie, hurrying to outpace the pain, no idea where he was heading.

Certain invisible wires were pulled to move his limbs in a certain direction.

This suffering of his was very great, no denying. It's an article of faith with him that when Alex says things he means them. So Jamie's rock and foundation is gone, his world is shattered, the ground has fallen away under his feet. Cliches, yes, and not ineffective, but, remembering my achievements *in the beginning*, you'll be expecting better from Mr Creativity.

Jamie has disappeared. Yellowed leaves in sunshine against a cold blue autumn sky are pure beauty that pierces—or *would* pierce, if there were anyone to pierce. Surprise occurs at the continuation of certain bodily and mental processes. The knowledge still operates that to walk, first this leg must move and then that one. There is a need to pee, not pressing. Here at the road roundabout is the sports shop with the assistant who looks like an intelligent rugby player and chats to customers as though selling is purely incidental. There's no-one to find him fanciable now. Once upon a time Isobel, Alex's mother, spending Christmas with a couple named Alex and Jamie, forgot to put in brandy when she made the brandy sauce and no-one liked to mention it: that's the sort of incident that in the telling gives happiness to a life, but now it's viewed from out in the street through an excluding window.

Jamie's impetus has dried up, he has come to a halt, he finds he's looking up at a tower like a squat dinky castle.

He's passed it innumerable times. (Well, I can number them, actually.)

Something is posted up on a board: "Come unto me, all ye that labour and are heavy laden, and I will give you rest." One of *my* invitations.

He flinches. Rest, the final rest he thought he'd found, has been destroyed by Alex's words.

Then—watch his face—he gives it a second thought, what he's read. It draws to itself similar phrases. Phrases picked up at school and Sunday school and Boys Brigade. Phrases gathered from choral music by Bach, Purcell, Handel, Elgar, etc, CDs being a very useful channel of unobtrusive propaganda. Phrases that hover in the culture, ready to make themselves heard. The phrases call like doves. Have you not known? Have you not heard? Has it not been told you from the beginning? Comfort ye, comfort ye…. He healeth those that are broken in heart: and giveth medicine to heal their sickness. He shall feed me in a green pasture; and lead me forth beside the waters of comfort. Art thou troubled? (People think that's religious because Handel set it to solemn music and it includes the archaic "thou" and Kathleen Ferrier sang it, but actually it isn't.) O rest in the Lord. Thou has been our refuge: from one generation to another. I am with you alway, even unto the end of the world.

Unlike fucking Alex.

The silence of an empty church—suddenly, oh, how it beckons. Jamie tries the door handle.

Normally we keep the doors locked because of vandals and suchlike. Beer cans and used condoms have been found in the pews. But for Jamie's sake, when the minister's wife went in to fetch the church dusters for washing, I had her forget to lock the door afterwards. Her husband will give her a row for that.

Jamie stands in the aisle. At the front there's a small round window that from the road looks like a porthole; from here it's the eye of a mosaic fish. He's isn't at all religious so he doesn't pray or anything. Even so, the woody silence inserts itself between him and his misery.

Good, good.

On an impulse—so he would call the little internal nudge I caused to arise—he flips open at random the top copy of a stack of Bibles. Why, there's Psalm 136. On Saatchi and Saatchi's advice, every second line flashes the same message: "His steadfast love endures for ever."

Such a contrast to a mere twenty years, Jamie.

And when a couple of pages fall back of their own accord (because of the binding, gravity, etc) I do my stuff again and guess what happens to leap out from Psalm 118?—"It is better to take refuge in the Lord than to put your confidence in man."

In the empty church Jamie is descended upon by the realisation that all the hopes and yearnings and trust and reliance that religious people invest in me, he has invested in Alex, with his faint deafness in one ear, his golf, his involvement in Amnesty International, his width (rather than paunchiness) that he tells Jamie with irritation he isn't *hiding* with his floppy shirts. It is to this Alex—a human being, for fuck's sake—that Jamie has been looking for the eternal, never-failing, ever-present, etc, love and strength and refuge that is available only from me. No way, baby!

My net is only inches away.

"But there's a problem," I hear you say. "You've already told us that Jamie isn't religious. He doesn't *believe*. So however much he aches for what you have on offer, he simply doesn't think it's there to be had. He may have laid up treasures on earth, where they rust and corrupt, but he doesn't think there are any treasures anywhere else. He's like someone browsing wistfully in an old mail-order catalogue when he thinks the company has gone out of business. You've forgotten the rock of his intellect."

The marshmallow of his intellect, more like. Of anybody's intellect. No problem there. Any moment now there will occur—well, nothing will *occur*, no flashes or visions, it'll just have become impossible for him *not* to think of the world as declaring the glory of me. As for his intellectual pride and his piddling need to believe he has not sold out, has not fooled himself, under the pressure of emotional need—oh, he'll tell himself something tricksy like this, that unless you believe, you can't understanding what it is you're rejecting, so his previous rejection wasn't really a rejection at all. Geddit?

There's a corner of the church reserved for 'business': piles of parish magazines, leaflets about this and that, a notice-board with lists and dates and rosters and events and special meetings. I manage to give a little shimmer— oh, nothing you could report as heavenly radiance pouring forth—to a notice about the minister being available for private counsel. How the 'phone number stands out!

Jamie, being intelligent, is aware that the minister will have gross personal characteristics. Tufts of nasal hair. A face lumpy from the effort of sublimating irritability into see-the-best-in-everybody love. The fact that his wife may be there in the bath next to the toilet-bowl doesn't prevent him going in and taking a shit. She has never really been able to reconcile herself to this, though she has never objected, having been bullied by him into thinking, with the front part of her mind, that it would be a denial of our full humanity, spirit and flesh combined, to do so. Jamie exalts in the thought that this gross specimen—and, face it, everyone is a gross specimen, even the minister's fragrant wife—will nevertheless be, by his private counsel, Jamie's route to the steadfast love endures for ever.

Jamie takes out his pen.

He's looking for something to write on, here's some leaflet with a handy blank space on it, he's inscribing the first digit of the minister's number.

Yes! I punch the air, so to speak.

The second.

The third.

Hey! He's screwed up the leaflet.

And he's put his pen away, he's turned, is walking…

Ah, he's turned back.

Oh, but it's only to pick up the screwed-up leaflet and throw it into the discreet bin in the corner.

Well, brownie points for you, tidy boy!

Now he's walked away completely, right out the door.

Look, sweetie, I didn't give you free-will for *this*!

Sometimes I wonder why I bother, I really do. I mean, he's only human, I'll get no steadfast love for ever and ever, etc, from him…

That fast stamping walk again, back the way he came. In the main door, up the common stairs one at a time but with rat-a-tat emphasis like drums heralding the big moment.

Into the flat. Straight into the toilet. A long pee.

That is *not* why he rushed home. This is no time to start fooling myself. Next move quick!

He's shaking his penis after peeing. I beam him the idea that it's utterly absurd to think that this organ, with its ugly excessive drooping foreskin, can have anything to do with securing himself the steadfast love that endures for ever.

Talk about about having ears to hear and not hearing. This is getting worrying.

He zips up, takes rather too long washing his hands as proof of sturdy independence of Alex, goes into the sitting-room. Alex, usually such a quick reader, is still occupied with *The Guardian*. I make Jamie's eyes prick with tears to distract him from drawing inferences from that.

Alex looks up, his face a mask of hello-you're-home politeness. It's a wall of skin within which Jamie can't detect love, pleasure in him, the upholding enfolding substance of his life. He thinks: My God, my God, why hast thou forsaken me?

Hey –those words came to him spontaneously! I'm still in with a chance!

While Alex says, with the impersonal obligingness that everyone gets from him, "Someone from your work 'phoned," I'm busy engineering a wrong number. It will just happen to be a clergyman. It would be going a bit far for it to be the very clergyman whose number Jamie nearly wrote down, but any clergyman might strike Jamie as Significant at this moment and tip the balance.

"Thanks."

"Frances. I wasn't sure when you'd be back so I couldn't tell her when to 'phone again." Alex speaks as though Jamie has been out on some normal errand like walking the dog of old Mrs McBride, who lives in the flat downstairs and has arthritis, though it's a fat plodding peke, no fun to walk, and Mrs McBride always behaves as though she's doing them the favour in letting them take it.

Da-*da*! There's my wrong number, my *clerical* error (ha!). Alex says, "That could be her ringing back," but he says it as though mentioning a curious fact for contemplation only, like the number of years it takes for light to get from Sirius to earth, absolutely nothing to do with the shrill imperative ringing out.

Jamie makes no move to answer it. It's rung, what, ten times already.

Am I losing my touch?—something else—anything—

The hairs bunch from Alex's nostrils, luxuriant, oddly crimped like they've been caught in something. Pretty revolting. Well, I managed to change world history by the length I gave to Cleopatra's nose, so this has got to have potential for helping a frigging human relationship down the tubes.

Go on, Jamie, notice his nostrils as never before, be *very* revolted.

Jamie, I'm talking to you.

I kill the 'phone.

Please, Jamie.

Jamie stares at Alex. Alex lowers his eyes to his newspaper—he's dismissing Jamie?—I snatch at hope— no, it's a sort of soul-gathering prelude. Shit. Alex performs the action of someone slowly raising his eyes from his newspaper. Their eyes meet and hold.

CRISPIAN AND HIS KIND

"You're being rung up from Germany."

She calls it out to the garden, without the amicable preface of his Christian name and without any attempt to locate him. She's using the dead voice with which she so often addresses him and which informs him she is excluding resentment from it. The sultry air deadens it still more. Also absent from her voice is any expression of interest in the fact of his being telephoned from Germany the day after the ultimatum about Poland. As he emerges from the cluster of box trees which he's been trying to shape into a concealed enclave for the limestone kissing-seat, Patricia is already re-entering the house.

Not even troubling to address him over her shoulder, she adds into the open doorway of the house, "It's Hartmut Brandt."

No, her impassive tone did not take on an overlay of accusation for the last three words. Relief at this causes a sense of something odd about those three words to vanish.

In his study, which before their marriage she had declared would be the nursery, a playful declaration of intent to take over both his house and him that for a time he had found reassuring, he adopts his official voice. "Hyde-Harrington here."

"Crispian! It is so good and nice to hear your voice. So much time has been passing."

He resists the impulse to correct *has been passing* to *has passed*. Once he would not have resisted, as he did not resist other temptations.

"Who is that?"

"Here is Hartmut."

"Hartmut who?"

"Crispian, I think you wish to make jokes? That is your English humour? In Berlin, we were close friends, one year close friends. You have to remember me, no, you must remember me, that is the right English?"

"I understand your English but not, I'm afraid, what you are talking about." After a pause not long enough to permit an answer, he adds, "But one knew so many people in Berlin, pupils and so forth. Look here, suppose we did know each other—meet—when I was in Berlin." Anyone overhearing that last sentence would think that politeness alone, entirely unsupported by memory, prompted him to utter it. "What's this about, your telephoning me? My wife called me in from the garden to speak to you." His tone says that a major sacrifice has been made to facilitate a conversation which, so far, has been entirely profitless.

"Your wife? Ah, you also."

"One usually marries."

"I promise to you that I have said to her only my name, not information."

Suddenly, Crispian knows what was odd about Patricia's last three words, *It's Hartmut Brandt.* That's how you'd refer to a mutual acquaintance; at least, to someone whose name you were both familiar with. Wouldn't a person who had never heard of Hartmut Brandt—and, most certainly, Crispian has never mentioned him to her!—have said, "Someone called Hartmut Brandt"?

"Look here, this is all Greek to me. An idiom meaning I don't understand at all. Now why don't you tell me, very clearly, why you are ringing me up?"

"Well, my friend, my very dear old friend, we must

speak, if wife or not."

"Indeed." Light irony.

"You and I, both in country's *Ministerium*—you would say, both are in ministry of government? We can be the way for saying important things."

"I can't think what."

"This demand of your Prime Minister Chamberlain and France that Germany shall withdraw from Poland. It is foolishness."

"Indeed." Light irony again.

"It is necessary to understand that such a demand cannot be accepted—agreed—what is the word?"

It is necessary to—the phrase that Hartmut adopted from him, over-using it until it became their intimate joke in the little room in the Durlacher Strasse behind what had once been the studio of a famous artist. Hartmut using it again and again as he makes the *Eintopf* stew which will last them three or four days, replenished with more ingredients as it diminishes in the pot, and their use of the phrase in bed, causing laughter...

The voice is continuing, "It is necessary to understand that the Führer cannot, when it is demanded in the front of the world, withdraw our forces. He would lose his face."

"Lose face. Look here, why are you telling me this? It's a matter to be communicated through the usual diplomatic channels."

"Ah, what a government will say to the other, over the diplomatic channel, can be to pretend, deceive, to act the part. May be said under the eyes of the world, and so not speaking with freedom. Crispian, it is true that you also work in a *Ministerium* as I do?"

"I am a civil servant in the Colonial Office. I have

nothing to do with Poland." No disclosing of secrets there.

"Even though, but it is possible, yes, for you to transfer...to transmit—the word is right?—a message to Prime Minister Chamberlain?"

"*Convey* would be better. I am afraid I cannot help you."

"Even though, permit me to say the message, my dear Crispian. The Führer will ignore your Prime Minister's demand. He can do nothing other, it is necessary one must understand that. But it is his word of honour that if England and France do not declare the war, our forces from Poland will withdraw after six weeks only and he will hold a speech to tell the world he is persuaded to peace from your wise Chamberlain. This I tell you, am telling you, with highest authority. Highest."

To say that Chamberlain, too, will want not to lose face and that Hitler cannot be trusted to honour his word of honour would risk being construed as falling in with this back-door approach and entering into negotiations. "I can only repeat that any message your government may wish to send to my government must be conveyed through the usual diplomatic channels."

"Crispian, oh my dear friend, it is necessary to understand what the war will bring with it. Berlin will be destroyed."

Berlin will be destroyed!

"Our Berlin. All in ruins, the places where we were, you and I. The room that was ours in house where was former the studio of Ludwig Kirchner. Bar Zum kleinen Löwen will be destroyed, where was our meeting. The Hotel Strandschloss, where we first found to love, after our voyage on steamboat on the Müggelsee."

"I think you must be confusing me with someone else.

Good morning." Crispian says it, not just to Hartmut, but to anyone who might be imagined having overheard the conversation. His manner of replacing the receiver, shaking his head as he does so, his face a mask of dismissive puzzlement, demonstrates to the watching world that he has been on the receiving end of incomprehensible nonsense, nothing more.

He finds her in the day sitting-room. She has been reading the *News Chronicle*, its front page heavy with crisis. Her face, with its domed forehead and thin, emphasised, almost semi-circular eyebrows, is as immobile as the face on a child's doll. He is made aware that it is poised between two possibilities. It might relax into comfortable smiling acquiescence in being the wife who tends the flowers, supervises the daily helps and the gardener, and arranges evenings of bridge at which (though he has not witnessed this for himself, for work so often keeps him at his pied-à-terre in London) she is an excellent player. Or the face might crack open in an explosion of madness or violence.

"A work matter," he says, a phrase normally effective in allowing him to say no more.

Now, however, a look of expectation enters her face and raises the fine semi-circular eyebrows, as if this time the phrase can be nothing but the prelude to disclosing full details. Surely she could have overheard nothing to justify her strange air of being entitled to information.

Ah, he did mention *my wife*; though even if she was eavesdropping, he had shut the study door, which should have been sound-proof...

Diplomatic compromise.

"Someone who says he remembers me from my year in Berlin. Now works in some government ministry and knows I do and thinks we can sort out the Polish business between us. Some rambling sentimental farrago which I couldn't follow. Probably drunk. Shows what a funk they're in."

She folds the newspaper and sets it down, as though something makes it her business, as much as his, to decide what is to be done.

"I suppose"—but he's already shaking his head at what she's about to say—"you should report it. There might be something in it. At the least, it's evidence of the mood in Germany."

She persists, "Why not?"

"For goodness' sake! Some crazed German I may have met just once. It's not worth a moment of anyone's time."

She nods sympathetically. "I suppose if you reported it they might wonder how you came to know such a person and might think you knew him rather well if he takes the trouble, years later, to find out that you are a civil servant and get hold of your number at home and ring you up." Her voice has lost its dead tone and is entirely comradely. Her eyes as are innocent as the garden visible through the French windows, a free informal garden, silently absorbing the sunshine, carefully tended.

Who was the Roman senator who ended every speech with 'Carthago delenda est,' Carthage must be destroyed? Berlin must be destroyed!

He replies, "Exactly. It's in neither of our interests to rock the boat, putting questions in people's minds." He moves his head in a wide sweep as if the walls of the day sitting-room are transparent and permit a survey of the luxurious home he provides for someone whose father committed suicide after losing all his money in the slump; someone who then lived a ramshackle hand-to-mouth existence, passed around among relations, forced to abandon her degree at Girton because the money had gone; someone who has always seemed grateful that he decided she would make him a suitable wife. "Nothing to be afraid of, of course."

"No, of course not. Though," she adds, "someone might have been listening. Oh, not MI5." She laughs at the possibility. "But Ada Greave at the post office exchange—everyone says she eavesdrops when she connects people, and she has a loose tongue. She told Dolly Messiter that Laura Jesson's husband has been seeing a woman in Rye called Hilary." Anyone eavesdropping now on him and Patricia would think this was just the intimate gossipy talk of a husband and wife on excellent terms. She even giggles, prelude to sharing an absurd thought. "Hilary's a name a man can have as well as a woman, isn't it? So it might even be a man Fred's seeing!"

He is trying to shape an appropriate half-smile that unites amusement with disgust, when she adds, "I didn't know you spent a year in Berlin."

Berlin will be destroyed!

"You must have forgotten."

"No, you didn't tell me." Her voice is combatively sure. She stands up to fuss over some pink dahlias in a bowl. "You told me you went to Berlin with some rowers from your college for a rowing match against students over there. You beat them hollow and met Goebbels, who was a relation of one of them."

"How extraordinary if I didn't mention it. Well, after the rowing, I decided to stay on for a bit—I'd just graduated—people, the fellows I was rowing against, seemed nice. One of them invited me to, as a matter of fact. To stay with his family."

"And that was Hartmut Brandt?"

"I don't remember—"

"You don't remember the name of the person in whose home you lived for a year?"

"Of course I do. What I meant was, I don't remember ever meeting this Hartmut Brandt." He is maintaining the genial tone appropriate to husband and wife having a perfectly friendly conversation; yes, it's perfectly friendly. "But then, you're bound to meet the odd fish or two when you teach English for a year." He looks interestedly towards the French windows. "No thunderstorm yet. That was the weather forecast, wasn't it? I'll get back into the garden while I can. I know Binks complains I don't do things correctly, but it's awfully satisfying after a week's work at a desk in London, and if a man can't work in his own garden—"

"You gave English lessons?"

"It was a way of getting ready cash to pay the rent. Cash for everyday expenses."

"Like Wys and Chris."

"Who?"

"That's what Veronica calls them. They're writers. They were at one of her firm's publishing parties, one of the ones she took me to. W.H. Auden, he's quite a famous poet, very modern, and Christopher Isherwood. They were talking about when they were teaching English in Berlin."

So she could have heard of Hartmut Brandt before. Hartmut meeting these writer chaps in Berlin—perhaps even in Zum kleinen Löwen, that he'd been so sentimental over; and then these writers being introduced to a woman called Hyde-Harrington at Veronica's firm's party and asking whether she's a relation of the Crispian Hyde-Harrington mentioned as his very dear friend by a Hartmut

Brandt they knew in Berlin...

"From all that they said, it sounded to me," she says carefully, ceasing to fiddle with the dahlias, burying her nose in them, sniffing with an air of ecstasy that isn't like her at all, "as if it wasn't English they were teaching but Greek. Or perhaps it was that they were learning Greek."

Berlin will be destroyed!

"I'm still not convinced that this strange German ringing you up shouldn't be reported," she says, impertinently but entirely ingenuously. Her face and her voice and the eyes beneath the semi-circular eyebrows show no present awareness that her sister's boss in the publishing firm has a brother who is a Parliamentary Under-Secretary of State at the Foreign Office and that to this brother Patricia could readily transmit a message about her husband receiving strange telephone calls from Germany.

Sometimes in diplomacy it is necessary to cede territory. He makes his bid in a voice warm with fond reminiscence that does not falter even at the sudden recollection that dahlias, so ecstatically sniffed, have no smell. "I was remembering, while I was on the telephone, how you threatened to take my study for a nursery."

Her voice snaps out of spousal amity into tartness. "It would have been a waste of time, had I done so."

"Still plenty of time." Warm fondness maintained.

War will not be prevented. Everyone will be shaken up, plunged into new courses, creating new patterns of life, new patterns of themselves, out of the wreckage of these bleak and anxious years. If war gives grounds of fear, there are also grounds of hope. Who knows what new currents might not flow when he braces himself for the supreme effort that will be demanded? Who knows what he might, so gratefully, be jolted into?

Patricia being literary and intellectual—it was English she was reading at Cambridge, wasn't it, before she had to leave?—he offers a sort of mental caress. "That Brandt fellow was getting extraordinarily maudlin about times spent with whoever he thought I was. That's the trouble with German Romanticism: it too easily topples over into greasy sentimentality."

...Could Hartmut may have slept with one of these writers?

Even with both?

Berlin will be destroyed!

Patricia's response comes with a smile that could easily be one of delighted tenderness. "You may be right. One of the things people don't know is that Goebbels is a specialist in Romantic literature."

"Well, it's necessary for everyone to buck up, now, and settle down to the realities of life."

"The realities of life," she murmurs. No, not a wry comment addressed to the gods; just an artless expression of dawning happiness.

He is pleased to discover that alongside revulsion towards the old world that will be destroyed, he is being taken over by hope and even confidence. Her cream cotton day-dress—it has a small faint green-and-maroon floral motif—is limp in the summer heat and the buttons all down the front proclaim its ready removability; nevertheless he takes her in his arms. Although the dress has shoulder-pads that keep his fingers at a distance, he caresses into one of her shoulders, or tries to, all the electricity of a shoulder in a rough shirt in the Durlacher Strasse.

He murmurs back, "And it isn't necessary to pass on

that silly message. It would just make things worse. Give Herr Hitler longer to entrench himself in Poland while they all fuss about what it means. Don't you agree?"

He adds, "Darling?"

"Of course I do, darling." Her face is nothing but wifely love and acquiescence.

The kiss he gives her would surely convince an onlooker that passion is breaking forth; is so convincing as a kiss that one attends inwardly and hopefully for signs that it does indeed spring from passion. Tenderly, as though it were a sweet nothing, he says, "Peace for our time."

She has pulled back. Her face is again hard and immobile like a doll's, but her stare informs him that he is now the one whose face is poised between two possibilities—poised between smiling upon his wife like a normal competent husband and cracking open in an explosion of madness or violence.

In her dead voice she says, "Why on earth are you talking like Mr Chamberlain and Munich?"

Her voice relaxes into tentative understanding. "You mean you've changed your mind?—Hartmut Brandt's message might preserve peace and you've decided to report it?"

"Oh, no, no, Patty. I meant, peace for you and me. For the rest of the world, I'm afraid it's war."

Berlin will be destroyed!

HUMAN RELATIONSHIPS
UNDER CAPITALISM

"—*BEWARE OF ADDERS*," cries Simon, interrupting himself in mid-rant. "Did you see that notice?"

"Stop the car!" he insists in an irritated voice, as though he'd already said it once and been ignored. He's already out of the car as Barratt eases it onto grass and halts.

*   *   *

Driving south along the single-track Glen Gairn road had been a nervous negotiation of blind summits and concealed twists. Passing places demanded notice in case oncoming traffic, visible only at the last moment, threatened a head-on crash. But you also grew aware that the road was running high and the landscape had opened up like the heart can do. The smooth terrain descended westward in sunshine to motionless miniature distances, then rose to new heights, new enigmas, though there had been safe insulation in a news programme on the car radio and Simon's equable commentary on it.

"Market forces," went an interviewed voice, "can't any longer be left in control of our social and economic landscape. The credit crunch made *everyone* realise that."

"Not me," Simon replies cheerfully, in keeping with the fact that his red hair retains the sharp red of a young boy's instead of having sobered into the dirty brown appropriate to middle age. He still has the leanness of body, too, but also the freckles. He has accumulated 522 friends on Facebook.

"When this country," says the voice with unpractised sincerity, "decided that each person going all-out for his own private profit was the best way to advance the common good, the country bought an old wives' tale with no more credibility than the idea that you can't get pregnant the first time."

"Nice," says Simon in unfeigned admiration of the wit of the comparison, but he continues immediately: "So it's to be tax rates at 95% again, state control of every fucking thing, and we've all got to get teary about the so-called needy—"

He's jolted by a sudden swerve for which there's no obvious reason. "—Careful!—the fucking so-called needy who only need to get up off their arses and *do* something instead of taking the easy option of dependency culture. And the *government* running industry, for God's sake. Destroying us. Squeezing us out."

"The anaconda of the state," says Barratt loyally, and he has every reason to mean it because their business— signing up and hiring out nurses—has gone down the pan after the National Health Service set up its own nurse banks and also started getting picky about the qualifications of agency nurses, even though most of them had been trained by the NHS in the first place.

The rounded snout of a ridge appears across the valley, an imagined hillside in a sixteenth-century painting, tiny trees cresting it as though marching to something good, perhaps to a bower where gods and men dwell in perfect harmony.

"The anaconda of the state." Barratt said it not only

loyally but gratefully, too, since Simon hasn't mentioned Barratt's guilt lately. Barratt knows he'd wasn't a good businessman, too timid or something, too little drive or self-esteem. "It's just...," he'd say, petering out, or "But what's the use?" Simon, incomprehending, had demonstrated time and again how a nursing agency was to everyone's advantage, the NHS able to call on extra nurses precisely when it needed them, the nurses—many of them single mums—welcoming the flexibility of not being shackled by fixed hours and a permanent contract of employment, and themselves rightly rewarded by 33% commission for their initiative. He'd rebuked Barratt: "Your parents wouldn't have had any sentimentality about it. They bought their council house as soon as Mrs Thatcher freed them to and sold it on at a good profit."

"And fucking unions," Simon continues as Barratt slows for a lamb that seems not to know which side of the road its mother is on and runs from side to side bleating, "holding the country to ransom with their so-called demands, no heat or light in the depths of winter because the miners or electricity workers or some other load of shits are holding the country to ransom, exploiting people's basic needs to get more money...I *remember* those nights in the 70s without electricity, Barry." He says the last bit as though he never mentioned it in the nineteen years they were together. "Doing my school homework by candlelight. The exercise-book caught fire."

"Demands," says Barratt.

"What?"

"They were demands, not so-called demands." But this dig is ingratitude, given that Simon hasn't for a long while now alluded to the blameworthy things Barratt did like telling hospitals that Nursing Help Service (Scotland) wouldn't claim the whopping introduction fees that its terms and conditions allowed it to charge when hospitals gave permanent jobs to people who'd first been supplied on an agency basis. Barratt says, "Fucking pillocks," nodding towards a red Skoda on their left. In his heavy sagging face the lips remain cherubic, unfit for swear-words. "Parking in a passing place. They could cause a fucking accident."

Two women in thick old-fashioned blue shorts made purely for use and not for style, so their white legs look stringy and unfeminine, are ascending the hillside above the Skoda. They hold tall staves, not modern walking poles.

"It wasn't a passing place. It was off the road," Simon retaliates for Barratt's little dig about *so-called*, which obviously came from lingering resentment because Simon, as he had a perfect right to, had ended the relationship after the business failed. When Simon could feel they were a pair of buccaneers in alliance, engaged in the war of all against all for the world's booty, everything was fine between them. It had been flattering, a testimony to Simon's own power, to think of Barratt as an independent operator who'd hooked up with him just because it was profitable to Barratt to do so. The charge between them was even enhanced, at least on Simon's side, by awareness that they could have been business enemies.

But when financial disaster came and they learned that the Edinburgh house in Easter Belmont Road for which they'd triumphantly paid a million and a half needed to be sold to pay debts, Barratt had felt like a liability, too. "We've still got each other," Barratt said, but Simon, wriggling out of his arms, had to explain that they were no longer partners in any meaning of the word.

He'd said, "You invested too much in the relationship, Barry. You've got to cut your losses and move on. You're too dependent, Barry. Needy."

As Barratt noses the Volvo across the steep old hump-backed bridge over the Gairn at the heart of the glen, immensely picturesque though not built to be picturesque, Simon can still admire his own wit when, having begun sleeping with a nurse who wore nothing under his scrubs, he'd described it as "salvaging one of the firm's assets". He'd been pleased that Barratt fell into the spirit of the thing, telling people even in Simon's presence, "He's trading me in for a younger model," and on one occasion Simon replied, with a thrilling realism which created a sort of intimacy of its own, "You'd have done the same except that a pot belly is not a commodity for which there's much market demand." And Barratt had even continued the joke, replying, as he slapped his belly, "Too much of a competitive edge." But the luxury country-house hotel wouldn't let them cancel their booking even though circumstances had changed, and the small print outrageously allowed the thieving bastards, who had taken credit card details along with the booking, to charge the full cost even if they didn't turn up, so Simon had decreed going ahead with the holiday anyway. "Just as friends," he'd warned.

Now a different radio voice is responding to the earnest one to ensure balance, a statesman's public voice tuned to public truth, making private thoughts feel impertinent and helpless.

"The *right* course of action has to be taken. That is essential to our country's future. What Victoria would like is to turn the clock back to socialism, but the hard-earned experience of the last half-century is that socialism is a failed experiment. Eastern Europe was our laboratory. We *know*, know on the basis of irrefutable evidence, what happens when bureaucrats interfere in the natural processes of wealth creation, in the free market. Competition, hard but fair competition, forces up quality and forces down prices, and stifling it is an attack on prosperity and freedom *for all*."

"Not to mention," says Simon comfortably, "an attack on my, our, everyone's right to do what they want with their *own* money instead of having it *stolen* by the state and handed out to people for whom living on benefits is a lifestyle choice, the feckless and the scroungers and the idiot thirteen-year-old girls who can't wait to be 'single mums' like their mothers and grandmothers. The so-called needy. *So-called* used correctly there. And—*BEWARE OF ADDERS*. Did you see that notice? Stop the car!" He's already out of the car as Barratt eases it onto grass and halts.

* * *

In the silence a lark sings and they remark almost in chorus, "The Lark Ascending," this being the name of a piece of music that, they have read, accumulated most votes in a poll to decide the nation's most in-demand piece of classical music

"*BEWARE OF ADDERS*. That's amazing," says Simon, touching the anonymous words, crude as a blackmailing letter, hand-painted on a board nailed to a post. "Why would someone put up a notice like that?" He looks at Barratt as though for answer, an entirely unrehearsed survival of their nineteen-year relationship, but continues, "I know. It's an attempt by some sheep-shagging farmer to scare people off his land. He doesn't like it that we've got the right to roam now and this is him trying to deny us our rights."

The notice stands sentinel before a gully and naturally makes one think of the path up through it as *snaking* upwards through the bracken and heather and blaeberry bushes, all motionless in the sun, no waves in them to mark the passage of slithering serpents. The lark sings on.

"Or perhaps," Simon goes on, "it's because of people parking in the passing places. To make them terrified to stop anywhere."

Barratt says, "But perhaps there *are* adders and someone is just being a nice guy, trying to warn people—"

"Barry, *there are no fucking adders.*" Simon's spurt of rage is understandable because Barratt's business inadequacies mean that has no right to suggest Simon is mistaken. "It's just someone taking pleasure in frightening people. Someone trying to intimidate other people. Well, he's not intimidating *me.*" And in his trainers (Diesel Black Gold Positive Military, £120) he begins a sort of hop-step dance in among the clumps of heather and bracken and blaeberry bushes. "No fucking adders here."

Barratt watches him as though he's to give him theatrical notes on his performance. He says, "But aren't they timid? Won't all that clumping about just drive them away anyway?"

Without ceasing his hop-step Simon tugs off trainers and socks.

"Bare feet…. That'll hurt."

"Not a bit! No fucking adders here!"

And then he peels off his t-shirt (Westwood Gold Graphic, £97) and like one sort of stripper twirls it over his head and flings it aside. Barratt finds he's looked to see

PAUL BROWNSEY

if Simon's back has a dark zig-zag down it, as adders' backs
do. Simon dances on, then hurls himself onto the heather
and commences rolling about, this way and that, throwing
himself up and down and over and around, sending into
the air sun-warmed puffs of earthy or vegetable particles.
"No fucking adders here!—Aaauuh!" The yell is triggered,
not by a snake, but by a grouse suddenly shooting up with
its accelerating cry like a guttural motor, and in reply,
Simon, on his feet again, peels off the combat trousers
(Maharishi £150) and underpants (Dolce and Gabbana
£26.72) and his Red Indian dance is now entirely naked
and he's whooping, "No fucking adders here!" as he slowly
circles back towards Barratt.

There's a slablike outcrop of rock, scaly with grey-black
lichen, and in sudden exhaustion Simon sits down, then
leaps up again, not because he's lowered his arse onto a
serpent basking in the sun, as they are said to like to do,
but because the rocky sharpnesses hurt his buttocks.
Barratt has been moving about in the heather and bracken,
gathering up the abandoned garments, stamping his feet to
drive away adders before cautiously and quickly reaching
for each item. He hands the t-shirt to Simon, who throws
it under himself and sits again. Awkward with the
remaining clothes, Barratt tries to sit on the slab, too, but
the angle and shape make this difficult and he can sit only
back to back with Simon.

The lark is singing again, or perhaps it always was, or
perhaps it's a different one; no, there are two, three, and
there's a faint deep background hum as though stillness is
being made audible by sunshine. Barratt stares towards a
clump of pink-purple blossoms with the artificial
brightness and homogeneity of something dipped in
industrial dye: bell heather among the common heather. A

kind of peace settles, the churning up of the vegetation by Simon's dance might never have happened, and the land in its heights and distances is benign. "The power of nature," murmurs Barratt, incurious about the camouflage-like patchwork of different greens and browns on the hills that results from annual burnings dictated by grouse-rearing for the shooting industry. As for the ruined cottage just discernible in a sheltering dip of the land, easier testimony that this landscape has been shaped by generations of people making a living—well, it's a *ruined* cottage, merely picturesque; nature is reclaiming dominion.

And as they sit silently, back to back, sweaty Simon, recovering his breath, feels smarting and throbbing up through his naked body what he was oblivious to during his dance, namely, all the multifarious pains from scratches and scrapes and sharp poking digs. Feeling, too, the hard line of Barratt's belt (Mac's Handystore, £3-99) against his back, he experiences an erection founded on awareness of Barratt, the first since the business failed, despite the past week of sharing a bedroom with him. As though Barratt senses this, he reaches behind him and awkwardly pats one of Simon's self-marketing enterprises, a very incomplete six-pack.

"You're too needy," Simon says.

"Too right." But the hand stays put; stays put in supplication.

Or *is* it supplication?

Yes, Barratt's emotional dependency is no advantage, a fetter, something to shrink from. Yet it could also be said that he has been playing a long game to repossess the asset he wants, namely, himself, Simon, enduring all sorts of, well, cruelties until the moment is ripe for the merger. Even his acquiescence there in his own neediness—"Too right"—was a clever move in the struggle by a something that's independent, scheming, self-moving, relentless, willing to admit to anything to get what it wants. In the right light—in this unclouded sunlight, for instance, that bakes all fret and pretension out of the landscape—Barratt has something that looks alluringly like power.

On their awkward rock Simon swivels on his tee-shirt and takes Barratt, still clutching Simon's clothes to him, in his arms as best he can and kisses him passionately.

The trainers drop. Barratt pulls away. "No, look, I don't…" The sweet warm crushed smell of bracken drifts over them. He's bending to right the trainers, placing them neatly side by side. "I don't want it to be only, like, here and now. Because, like, you suddenly fancy open-air sex."

Simon admires this move. He's read somewhere that Richard Branson, just when people think they've got a contract sewn up with him, suddenly reopens a point they thought was settled and gets new concessions out of them, which is perfectly natural, evolution teaching us that people are always out to get advantage for themselves and put one over on competitors: the struggle for existence, the selfish gene, etc. Counting the times he's met Richard Branson, he says "Okay" before he realises he was going to say it.

"And Desmond?" Barratt ventures: "The scrubber in scrubs?"

"I'll let him go."

But Simon's not so weak he couldn't have held out for a better deal from a clingy person who always gave more in the relationship than Simon did; a person who's blameworthy, too. Simon shakes his head, sighs, looks at Barratt tolerantly. "Never really lived up to the significance of your name, did you?"

This alludes to the fact that, parents having the right to call children anything they want to, the children being *theirs*, he was named after his parents' aspiration to own a Barratt Home, of which there had seemed no hope in their council house back in the 1960s when his mother had been an assiduous visitor of show homes and had inaugurated a Barratt Home as the family's official dream.

"Named after a symbol of aspiration, and you couldn't hack it. Wouldn't push hard enough, not focused. Our business was perfectly legitimate, Barry. Perfectly legal. There was a market opportunity and we took it."

"All I can say is, I'm sorry," says Barratt ruthlessly.

Soon Barratt's clothes are off, too, and they are making love on their rock, but it's too hard and uncomfortable, and they slide down into the heather. There are in Simon the trembling beginnings of a new thought about *BEWARE OF ADDERS* but it is drowned by the distant first intimations of orgasm, and they are like two bees nuzzling the common heather, oblivious to landscape vistas that open up like the heart, but they are themselves observed, for two female hikers in blue shorts look down from above, their faces not shocked or amused or prurient but merely tender.

DAMAGE ENOUGH

No sign of him yet tonight. Of Rajiv. He needs a name, and Mrs Gandhi's sons give two to choose from. "Rajiv" has "raj" as a component syllable: rule, imperiousness, a superior being.

Sometimes Martin frowns at his watch and looks about conspicuously, exactly like someone waiting by arrangement for a taxi or friend: look, everybody, I have a perfectly legitimate reason for standing in the centre of Glasgow late at night. He keeps his eyes to himself. He is on the north side of St Vincent Street, opposite the toilets.

That Rajiv is Indian is a logical deduction. Only once has he been seen away from this web of streets converging on St Vincent Place. He came into the Waterloo, was halted immediately by the wall of eyes turned to appraise him. His Asian modesty had not bargained for this. He turned, was gone.

The deduction: Pakistanis are Muslims, forbidden alcohol, so they are less likely to go to bars, so Rajiv is Indian. There's an Indian beer, Cobra.

Martin rests one foot up against the stone balustrade behind him, fists in his jacket hand-rests. Once he followed Rajiv down to the urinals, stood next to him. He could have seen Rajiv's cock. But Martin just stared at the wall.

Rajiv must not think he's that sort.

Circumcision: is it an Indian thing?

Rajiv's face, he's studied that. As he strides by. It's a highly intelligent face, still something of the school swot in it. Sometimes a look about the mouth of too many teeth. Heavy black-framed glasses. He will be a mathematician or heart surgeon or nuclear physicist. Indian families nurture ambition in their children almost as much as Jewish.

A man has approached, hesitates. Balding. No, missing patches of hair—alo-something? Shabby fur-lined parka. That fat and wearing combat trousers! A face without hope. Here from habit, no more.

"Look, this is not a chat-up line."

Martin does not move even an eye muscle. Rajiv never speaks to anyone, let alone goes away with them. His fastidious Indian sensibility revolts at street pick-ups. Rajiv is a virgin.

The man nods towards two others standing at the incongruous wee tree by the toilets. "Look, those two are trouble." Under the streetlights they could be twins: hair shaved to bony stubble, black leather jackets, white shirts, what used to be called smart dress trousers. A couple with a lookalike thing? Looking for a threesome?

"Look, they aren't here for what we're here for." Pleading. No doubt it gives this no-hoper a kick to bracket himself with Martin: yeah, we're both contenders. He turns petulant: "Oh, please yourself."

He's here! Rajiv is striding from George Square, hands in the pockets of a long leather coat open and flapping. An expensive leather coat. Didn't some survey say that Asian kids have proportionately more mobile 'phones than any other section of the population? Rich Asian parents showering consumer goods on their offspring. In return for control. Rajiv needs rescuing.

Rajiv passes Martin without a glance. Deliberately without a glance, for he must know Martin by now.

Hey, given that Asian families are so controlling, how

come Rajiv can prowl the city centre night after night? *Where do you go, Rajiv?—Why are you so late, Rajiv?—Whom are you with, Rajiv?* Martin definitely hears that "whom": Indians' English can be better than the natives'. Rajiv has been brought up with English as his first language because he will need it to get on. Shrewd self-sacrificing parents. The large flat in Pollokshields has surprisingly ordinary furniture, even a chocolate-boxy picture of an Olde Englishe village, stagecoaches and crinolines, over the mantlepiece. There is not the faintest smell of curry.

Rajiv has come up from the urinals too soon for anything to have happened down there. He's looking about, frowning, to all the world someone unsure of his geographical bearings.

He crosses back to Martin's side of the street.

But he passes Martin without a glance again. Going back where he came from.

No, he's turned left into a shadowy lane. Making a wee circuit to bring him back to the toilets.

He's married, forced into an arranged marriage! That's why he can be out at all hours: Indian husbands are lords and masters, you read in *The Guardian* about wife-burning if the dowry is too small, he has no obligation to give his wife even a false story about where he is going.

Is a wedding ring an Indian thing?

Hey, the highest-proportion-of-mobile-'phones thing: Asian kids need them to call for help against racist attacks!

Rajiv a wife-burner? Come on! Rajiv's heart and mind are formed for the higher morality of his new culture.

Yep, here he is again, approaching the toilets down Buchanan Street. Something positively jaunty about him. Martin has a sudden picture of Rajiv striding between a row of beds, a long white coat in place of his flapping leather one. Of course! That is why he can be out and about: Rajiv is a junior hospital doctor. They work all hours (like his parents in their corner-shop), so he can come home any time of the day or night, be out days on end, and there will be no questions. Doctor Rajiv turning all the nurses' heads on the ward, male and female alike.

But he's off west along St Vincent Street, away from the toilets, away from Martin.

But his eye is caught by something in the window of John Smith's bookshop. So you'd say, the way he halts.

Martin's studies his watch one last time. Look, everyone: he's exasperated, he's finally given up on his delayed friend or taxi, he's going home, heading west, walking as fast as possible.

His eye, too, is caught by something in the bookshop window.

Martin and Rajiv stand side by side like men at a urinal, no peeping, eyes strictly on the books before them.

It's some back-to-classics promotion tied in with television serialisations: suave paperbacks of Fielding and Tolstoy and Balzac and, of course, lots of Dickens, Trollope, Jane Austen. Martin prepares a quip to open the conversation: Dickens is just Dickens, but everyone says Jane Austen, never just Austen, to distinguish her from that other great novelist, Kylie Austen.

That flatters Rajiv, the assumption that he'll get it.

What does Rajiv's brown mind make of these Bibles of an alien culture? Come to that, what does he make of his own culture of...well, many-armed gods dancing on one leg, paintings like cartoons with people in lascivious eye-contact, women in film posters looking vaguely tarty despite their saris, the men always on the tubby side (though Rajiv, naked, wouldn't have a spare ounce on him)? He's forever locked out from the subtle coded world of *Mansfield Park* and *Barchester Towers*. On his face there's always this tragic awareness of himself as a lost man, an empty vessel for cultures to clash and swirl in. He needs a guide, someone to give him direction.

In reflection, in the shop window, Martin's eyes and Rajiv's rise and finally meet.

He's off, back towards the toilets. Surely Rajiv doesn't *want* the move to be made there, he *can't*, Indians have a high moral sense.

No, he's turned down Buchanan Street.

Look, you're white, don't pretend you can fathom his feelings. And he'll be jittery about his job, too: Doctor Rajiv standing scared, no, with head held high, before a medical tribunal, struck off for cottaging, end of career...

Ah, dodged left into an alley. A cobbled lane leads back up to the toilets...

"Where'd that fucking Paki go?" The voice presumes Martin's complicity.

Martin says complicitously, "Into the alleyway leading to Royal Exchange Square." Odd, really, that shaven heads are so menacing. He adds, informatively, pointing, "On the left. Down there."

He calls after them, his voice now protective in compensation, "He's not a Paki."

The two men are running like characters in *Trainspotting*, they turn into the alleyway. Martin follows almost as fast, hunching himself and concentrating on his tip-toes to imitate invisibility, for they may not welcome a witness.

Rajiv is staring in a shirt-shop window in the same lost way he'd stared at European classic novels. Shirts, too, are Western, unnatural covering for Rajiv's chest...

Without pause or challenge the lookalikes cannon into

Rajiv, knock him to the ground.

…yet Doctor Rajiv striding through the wards in Indian dress, in Gandhi pantaloon drawers, skinny legs protruding—impossible.

The two men kick, kick. Rajiv tries to get up, is downed again by a kick in that mouth with too many teeth.

Martin watches.

The other sounds of the city have vanished, there are just thumps, kicks, stampings. Deafening sounds.

Martin watches.

The men are voiceless. So is Rajiv. The fatalistic Indian peasant lies down and dies, it is fate, karma, the will of…not Allah…Shiva?

Martin looks conspicuously at his watch: I'm waiting for someone, that's why I'm standing here.

Look at Martin happen to notice something going on in the alleyway shadows. He peers.

He peers harder.

He puts an expression of horror onto his face.

At the top of his lungs Martin cries, "That's enough. That's enough. Help, help! Police, police! Racist thugs are beating up an Asian man!"

The lookalike lovers pause, stare towards Martin. One of them gives Rajiv a final kick, taunting Martin. Then they're away, vanished through the arch to Royal Exchange Square.

Martin runs forward like a brave man, he is on his knees at Rajiv's side.

Rajiv's face is undamaged?

No, it's only the dim light and Rajiv's dark skin, there's blood welling from his mouth, some sort of mess in one eye socket, a mangling of flesh at the side of his jaw. Damage enough.

Damage enough for love.

Martin says, "It's all right, I'm a friend, you're safe, oh, you poor guy, those bastards, those utter shits." He forces an arm tenderly around Rajiv's shoulders. Martin winces like you do when someone says they caught their finger in the door. "No, lie still, you may have internal injuries, just wait, someone will call an ambulance, oh God, you were nearly another Stephen Lawrence, no, don't worry, I won't leave you, I won't leave you, Rajiv."

A hand amazingly like Martin's own, nails so neatly trimmed, moves gropingly. Rajiv's heavy black-framed glasses: Martin makes searching gestures with his free hand, proof that he's at Rajiv's service, but he's focussed on making out what Rajiv is trying to say through the mess of his mouth: "...not waiting...friends...did not speak..." The accent is pure Glasgow. Not the most refined Glasgow, either: the alien child coped with playground tormentors by taking on their voice. Protective colouring.

"Look, you need me, I'll help you, I'll guide you, with me you can make it in a hostile society. You poor guy, you've got it so much worse, you get the racism *and* the homophobia, all on *your* head, you must be a man in a million not to be driven crazy by it. So your family cast you off, don't worry, you'll always have me, I'll never let you down, you are the man I've been looking for, I know you're scared to come out, but don't be, trust me, I love you, Rajiv, I love you, yes, men can love each other like the greatest loves in history, like the emperor who built the Taj Mahal for his dead wife, that's how much I love you, Rajiv."

The little archway into Royal Exchange Square is a miniature Arc de Triomphe. Out in the visible bit of Buchanan Street people walk by beneath the streetlights on

eternally unknown business. If they glimpse something—
oh, just a couple of drunks or druggies. Back at the toilets
people will still be going down and up: hey, what happened
to the alo-something guy? As for the bookshop window,
perhaps he and Rajiv can read *Emma* or *Anna Karenina*
together, if his eye recovers enough. Of course, there will
be permanent damage.

IN TERRA PAX

Stevie lets Arthur hold his hand even though he doesn't hold it as a hospital patient should, like someone merely drawing human comfort from it. He holds it in a lover's way, caressing the knuckles with his thumb, stroking it with his other hand. He even kisses it. Arthur is, of course, exploiting the circumstances to force him to endure a public show of affection. Stevie notes the sly glances to check how he takes this. He calls up his resolution, all those years ago, that Arthur needed him; needed him to put up with his ways.

Actually it's all right, because the two beds opposite have been vacated since Stevie's last visit and the occupant of the third seems asleep. But the hospital's pious antiseptic smell, that normally draws forth your best self, all grateful and benign, is powerless to protect Stevie from the old tormenting thought: you *would have* left me.

Arthur's voice is for hailing someone across the street. **"DO YOU KNOW HOW I HAVE BEEN OCCUPYING MY MIND WHILE I HAVE BEEN LYING HERE AT DEATH'S DOOR?"**

Has his operation somehow reduced his ability to monitor his own voice-level? But he greeted Stevie normally enough when he arrived.

"I HAVE BEEN TRYING TO THINK OF THE PERFECT MASS." A bellow on the last word. **"MADE UP OF THE BEST BITS OF THE OTHERS."**

"I'm just here." Stevie's voice has shrunk to a compensating whisper. His wiry frame that's never filled out sufficiently is helpless. "There's no need to shout."

"FOR THE *KYRIE*, I THINK IT WILL HAVE TO BE BACH, DON'T YOU? THE B MINOR MASS. NO OTHER *KYRIE* TRANSPORTS US SO INSISTENTLY INTO THE HEART OF THE TRANSCENDENT." He eyes the next bed. **"WRITTEN, BY THE WAY, OR PERHAPS NOT BY THE WAY, BY A PROTESTANT."**

Another bellow on the last word. Only an archway separates this bay from a corridor patrolled by remorseless doctors and nurses on the look-out for things to reprehend. Whatever authority figure Arthur's shouting may draw, Stevie resolves not to withdraw his hand from Arthur's. Yet I know you *would have* left me, Arthur Molyneux, even though you never did and never threatened to and the time is long past when anything could prove it one way or the other.

"THE *GLORIA*. HMM. NOT THE ONE IN THE *CORONATION* MASS, WHICH SOUNDS AS IF MOZART IS YELPING WITH DELIGHT AT THE RANGE OF FRAGRANCES ON SALE IN JOHN LEWIS'S. NOT MACMILLAN'S, EITHER: SUCH A SCREECH OF A *GLORIA*, LIKE HE'S DISCOVERED SOMETHING NASTY IN THE WOODSHED. WELL, POOR BOY, HE DOES THINK OF HIMSELF HARD DONE BY, AS A CATHOLIC IN THE WEST OF SCOTLAND. AS IF CATHOLICS NEVER WENT IN FOR BIGOTRY THEMSELVES."

"*Please*, Arthur. Sh."

"He is," says Arthur, "only pretending to sleep. **IT IS IN FACT HARD TO THINK OF A *GLORIA* THAT DOES JUSTICE TO THE GLORY THAT IS ITS SUBJECT-MATTER. SO LET US HAVE A *GLORIA* THAT DOES NOT EVEN TRY TO DO SO, THAT BY ITS VERY SIMPLICITY CONVEYS GLORY ONLY IN ABSENTIA: THE *GLORIA* IN ARVO**

PÄRT'S *MISSA SYLLABICA*. THOUGH THE *IN TERRA PAX* MUST BE VIVALDI'S, OF COURSE, FROM RV 589: PEACE YEARNED FOR WITH AN ACHE TOO GREAT FOR THE SOUL TO BEAR; ALMOST."

His eyes are on the next bed again. The man wears heavy-framed glasses as he slumbers. They and the full head of springy black hair could belong to a swotty youth eager to tell you of his discoveries about life, but the face is also doughy with disillusion and endurance.

"AND FOR THE *QUI TOLLIS...* SOMETHING STARK AND STERN? FOR MOST DEFINITELY, STEVIE, YOU AND I HAVE SINS TO BE TAKEN AWAY, THOUGH NATURALLY THE BASTARDS INSIST THEY HATE ONLY THE SIN AND LOVE US SINNERS. AS THOUGH THERE WERE A DIFFERENCE, WHICH IN OUR CASE THERE CANNOT BE. THE PUCCINI? NO, TOO MUCH LIKE SOMETHING SUNG ON THE BARRICADES IN *LES MISÉRABLES*. LET'S NOT THINK ABOUT STERNNESS AND STARKNESS AND DEFIANCE. WE'LL HAVE THE *QUI TOLLIS* FROM HAYDN'S *PAUKENMESSE*. A WARM, COSSETING CELLO SOLO TAKES YOU INTO IT, AND HAVING YOUR SINS TAKEN AWAY IS LIKE EATING CHOCOLATES WITH BRANDY BY A FIRESIDE. PASS ME YOUR CHOCOLATE BOX, STEVIE."

The pyjamas on the man in the next bed: they aren't Paisley-patterned after all. The yellowish-brown blobs against a pale blue background are teddy bears.

"FOR THE *DIES IRAE*—FOR I DO NOT PROPOSE TO DISTINGUISH A REQUIEM MASS FROM YOUR COMMON OR GARDEN MASS, FOR EVERY MASS IS ABOUT DEATH—NOT THE VERDI, I THINK. IT HAS THE TERROR BUT IS TOO CRUDE, TOO EARTHBOUND."

Why is a middle-aged man wearing pyjamas in a child's

pattern?

"AND MOZART'S *DIES IRAE* IS JUST THE WAILING SOUNDTRACK TO *HELL—THE MOVIE*. NO, THE DURUFLÉ, I THINK. DURUFLÉ'S *DIES IRAE* HAS THE TERROR, FOR WHO CAN AVOID TERROR WHEN HE THINKS OF WHAT HIS LIFE HAS BEEN?"

He gives Stevie the sidelong glance combining suspicion with a knowing smirk that a quarter of a century before made it Stevie's mission to seek out the real person behind the rambling pontificatings about life and literature that were fuelled both by alcohol and by Arthur's conception of what his Irishness demanded of him. He takes Stevie's hand to his lips again and murmurs, "Of that terror you have been, for me, the sole assuagement. Indeed, YOU HAVE BEEN MY MASS. BUT THE DURUFLÉ *DIES IRAE* HAS SO MUCH MORE THAN TERROR: THE PROFOUNDEST COMPASSION. WHICH IS NOT ALWAYS DISPLAYED BY THOSE WHOSE OFFICIAL BUSINESS IS WITH THE MASS. IS IT?"

If the chance had offered, oh how swiftly you would have dumped me and got yourself a wife. A headship: far too visible a position to be occupied by a poof living with another poof.

"DURUFLÉ'S REQUIEM HAS THE FULL DISTILLATION OF THE TERROR AND THE COMPASSION THAT ARE, BOTH OF THEM, OUR HUMAN HERITAGE. BUT LIFE THROWS THEM AT US IN SUCH JUMBLES AND DILUTIONS THAT WE NEED THE MASS TO BRING THEM TO US IN THEIR PURE, PURE FORMS, AS IN DREAMS WE FEEL THE PURE FORMS OF THE EMOTIONS, WITHOUT DISTRACTION, DILUTION, OR MITIGATION." The voice sinks. "He's a priest, you see. And the Duruflé Requiem reminds me of something else.

While I have been lying here at death's door I have been thinking back over my life. Drawing up the accounts. Staring death in the face makes you like that."

Stevie is taken over by a memory. He's a boy, in the back garden on a snowy winter's day, clutching a fire-blackened tin can that his father has made into a hand-warmer by filling it with—could it really have been embers from the garden fire?—wouldn't they be so hot that the metal would scorch you?

Suddenly it is the priest who is warming his hands on the tin can.

"You are not listening to me, Stevie." Even now that Arthur is bedridden his stocky build and boxer's brutal face confirm Stevie's schoolboy immaturity.

"Sorry."

"What the in some lights youthful features of Father Mahony distracted you from was this question: why was I not a professional success?" The hand that does not hold Stevie's wags a finger. "I failed to become a head teacher because of the Duruflé Requiem."

A dramatic pause cues the general public to be startled and intrigued by the oracular remark.

"That Future Leadership in Education conference at Crieff I was summoned to after local government re-organization. Totally useless yack-yack-yack, of course, merely something to put on a CV, nothing whatsoever to do with the fire and magic of real teaching. To my certain knowledge every principal teacher who went subsequently became a head. *But!* I chose not to go. I knew there were, there are, things in life more important than career success. Or the salary that goes with it. And when I didn't go my card was marked. So no headship for me. I had integrity. **OH YES, WE CAN BE PEOPLE OF INTEGRITY,**

WHATEVER SOME MAY SAY.

"You will be wondering *what* was more important to me than career success." His stare invites Stevie to guess.

Stevie looks away and Arthur barks out a laugh. "Choral Union that weekend, the Duruflé Requiem. **FUCKED** if I was going to miss singing that."

It is, of course, perfectly natural that Arthur has been brooding on his old headship ambition simultaneously with its piercing Stevie again, for they are one flesh and therefore blessed or burdened by secret visitations of the same thoughts.

"NOW AS FOR THE *ET INCARNATUS EST*... YOU KNOW THAT THAT IS THE HEART OF THE MASS. WHERE GOD TAKES ON HUMAN FLESH OR, AS I PREFER TO SAY, HUMAN FLESH SHINES FORTH IN ITS DIVINITY. NOT MOZART'S SOPPY *ET INCARNATUS EST* IN THE C MINOR MASS, LIKE SOME INSIPID MAIDEN IN PASTORAL OPERA TRILLING ON ABOUT HOW HER SHEPHERD-BOY IS TRUE. WHICH, BY THE WAY, I SUPPOSE YOU ARE NOT BEING WHILE I LIE HERE SUFFERING. Now don't get sulky and protesting. That was said *solely* because we have a reputation to maintain for **RAMPANT PROMISCUITY.**

"HAYDN AGAIN, I THINK. DON'T YOU? THE *PAUKENMESSE* AGAIN. GOOD OLD HAYDN, WHO KNEW THAT DIVINITY BEING MADE FLESH IS A MIRACLE, YES, BUT A QUIET, HUMANE, PATIENT ONE, TO WHICH THE ONLY APT RESPONSE IS A MELTING OF THE HEART."

"Whereas it never melted your fucking heart that your headship ambitions would mean abandoning me," Stevie wants to say but doesn't.

"FOR THE *CRUCIFIXUS*: SOMETHING SEARING AND

AGONISED, OF COURSE. THAT IS SOMETHING WE CAN IDENTIFY WITH, STEVIE, FOR WE HAVE BEEN CRUCIFIED ENOUGH AND WOULD BE STILL IF THEY HAD THEIR WAY. HE WAS DESPISÈD, AS WE ARE BY HIS NIBS. I THINK THE *CRUCIFIXUS* FROM MOZART'S *TRINITY* MASS, K 167. THOSE THUMPS IN THE ORCHESTRA: CAN'T YOU JUST FEEL THE NAILS GOING IN?"

Suddenly Stevie knows why he's wearing teddy-bear pyjamas. It's a form of mortification. Prada shoes for the Pope out of the offerings of the faithful but no designer pyjamas for this man. He knows they make him, as a priest, look ridiculous, knows they lower him from his status and dignity, and he wears them just *because* they do. The priest has had to set aside self entirely to become a pure channel of judgement and absolution; and of something else, too, that has even more power than the hospital smell to elevate you hygienically above your shoddiness. Yet that sublime function is exercised by a man with this ordinary, warm, sour, body, and the paradox is proclaimed by his absurd choice of pyjamas. Does he have an erection when he wakes in the morning, like many men? But he could hardly proclaim that.

"AND WE'LL HAVE A *LIBERA ME*, THOUGH OF COURSE THERE IS ONE FORM OF LIBERATION THAT HIS KIND WOULD NEVER ALLOW. *LIBERA ME*. RELEASE ME. NOT THE ENGELBERT HUMPERDINCK VERSION. THE DURUFLÉ AGAIN, I THINK. THAT MAGICAL MOMENT WHEN THE GLOOMY UNGAINLY TUNE IS REPEATED AND THE HARMONY SHIFTS AND ALL WEIGHT FALLS AWAY AND YOU REALISE YOU HAVE BEEN IN PARADISE ALL ALONG..."

But there is no release from the thought that Arthur

would have left him. Arthur, with his over-large head and shock of hair that's been grey since his twenties, is not a being who is necessarily there, without the possibility of absence, as God would be if he existed. This fact about Arthur hollows out the world like a blown egg and spins the world a thousand times too fast and life flies off it and the universe dies.

"AND SO WE COME TO THE OLD GLASGOW BIDDY, AGNES DAY, AND HER POSH FRIEND FROM KELVINSIDE, DONNA NOBBS. OH, THERE'S ONLY ONE POSSIBLE *AGNUS DEI*, ISN'T THERE? BACK TO BACH. BACK TO THE B MINOR. AN IMMENSE DRAMA HAS BEEN PLAYED OUT, THERE IS UNSPEAKABLE GRIEF AND UNSPEAKABLE COMFORT AND IT IS ALL COMPRESSED INTO THAT ALTO SOLO THAT GOES DOWN, DOWN INTO THE DEPTHS THAT, ASTONISHINGLY, ARE NOT THE DEPTHS OF HELL BUT WATERS THAT HIDE AND CLEANSE AND RESTORE. YOU HAVE PARTICIPATED IN THE GREATEST THING IN THE UNIVERSE. NO, YOU ARE THE GREATEST THING IN THE UNIVERSE.

"YOU KNOW, STEVIE, SOMEONE OVERHEARING ME TALKING SO POETICALLY AND SEARCHINGLY ABOUT THE PERFECT MASS MIGHT THINK I WAS A ROMAN CATHOLIC."

"Uh…it's not really overhearing, Arthur."

"BUT IT IS ALL FALSE, THE MASS. EVERY WORD OF IT." Now he looks openly at the priest. 'NO BEING BORN OF A VIRGIN AND BEING SACRIFICED FOR OUR SINS AND RISING FROM THE DEAD AND SITTING ON THE RIGHT HAND OF GOD."

"Arthur, please stop." Stop pulling out the priest's life-support tubes.

"OH, THERE IS TRUTH IN THE MASS BUT IT LIES A BLOODY SIGHT DEEPER THAN ANYTHING EVER DREAMT OF IN THAT WANKER'S PHILOSOPHY."

"Arthur, *stop it*."

"ON SOME LIPS IT IS PROFOUNDLY TRUE BUT ON *HIS* LIPS EVERY WORD IS FUCKING BOLLOCKS."

"Arthur, if you don't stop I will leave you."

He adds, "I mean leave here, now. I mean it."

But that would abandon the priest more completely to Arthur's mercy.

Without for a moment abandoning the sotto voce that propriety demands in a hospital ward, Stevie blazes: "Look. Keyhole surgery on your gall bladder is *not* death's door. And I'll tell you why you never got your headship. Your *fucking* headship. Just remember the mornings I couldn't get you out of bed because you were hungover. There were *some* things you were willing to sacrifice to your career but booze wasn't one of them. And as for integrity...you told them a *lie*, that your mother was ill. Nothing about refusing to give up singing some requiem. Some integrity."

There is a darkening of the light. A pale woman in black with very red lipstick meticulously applied stands in the archway leading to their wee bay of beds. Her black coat—a black *fur* coat, needing such courage to wear it through the grubby streets outside this hospital—is open, revealing a shiny black dress with flared skirt. There is a little black pill-box hat with a half veil. She might be on her way to some society function in the 1950s.

But Arthur is staring at Stevie in prolonged appraisal. "Oh dear." He reaches for the spouted cup of barley water. He dribbles the liquid onto his pyjamas: his feebleness, his illness. "Integrity," he croaks, so softly that

Stevie's head is drawn very close, "is not the same as speaking truth, and can tolerate a lie if the lie secures you from the world's unjust displeasure and penalties, and may even"—a jabbed finger undermines the show of feebleness—"*demand* a lie, as when the world's warfare is against the deep heart's core. It is a mark of *shallow* people to believe that integrity must always manifest itself in declaring truth." His breath is lemony with barley water.

Their heads remain close as they watch her plumping up and rearranging the priest's pillows, talking softly to him. He bends forward at her behest: his face is engulfed by the fur coat and will be up against the stiff black bodice. Her movements waft across a perfume of transforming purity, nothing like incense. Notwithstanding her posh clothes she is all care. The fur coat billowing, she sweeps on her high heels to the sink in the corner, changing the water in the priest's jug, elegantly rinsing his glass. Droplets on the black fur, perhaps, but it's too far to see. There's a cheap grey plastic stacking chair at the bedside; as she tidies it away to the head of the bed her scarlet nails transmute it into an artefact of subtle avant-garde design fit for an art museum.

Arthur murmurs, "The cardinal's mistress. Perhaps not quite all of them go after little boys. No, the cardinal in drag. Come to instruct Father Mahony—pronounced *Maanee*, you know, not *Muh-hoe-nee*—in the latest anathemas he is to issue against me and you and all our kind. Not his housekeeper, for sure. Nothing like Mrs what's-her-name in *Father Ted*. And not a nun, dressed like that. Mrs Doyle. And yet why not a nun? Can you be sure, these days? Lesbians have been observed wearing frocks."

He is watching Stevie's still-affronted face. He cajoles:

"May there not be an order of nuns that dresses like society women of the 1950s? Founded by Evelyn Waugh."

Eventually Stevie meets his eye. "The *Rich* Clares instead of the Poor Clares."

Now the sidelong appraising look is accompanied by a smile. "Excellent!" cries Arthur, and they laugh together, much more than the joke warrants, and, as often when Stevie is suffused by delight at Arthur's manifest approval, the thought comes to him that while Arthur got a third in English Literature, he has a Ph.D, albeit in maths. He discovers with pleasure that at no point has he withdrawn his hand from Arthur's.

"I see you can talk normally enough when I'm here. Less of the shouting, *if* you please." She stands at the entrance to their bay. She's short and wide and her pale grey smock and trousers, tight across a protruding stomach, mark her out as official, though there are so many kinds of auxiliaries and specialists and administrators in hospitals these days that heaven knows what her status is. Close-cut no-nonsense grey hair, glasses enhancing large penetrating eyes.

"Sorry," says Stevie.

Her answering smile is tight and formal. She pauses in her departure to nod at the grey plastic chair at the head of the priest's bed. "Put *them* in water."

Stevie has jerked to his feet, obedient like a long-limbed puppet, before he sees the spray of white lilies on the chair. The woman in black is gone.

"There's a vase down behind the sink," Arthur says in an elaborately repentant whisper designed to placate anyone overhearing it.

Surely lilies like these, faultless as another world,

breathing coolness like air-conditioning in the overheated ward, didn't come from the hospital shop. The inner trumpet is free of the stain of pollen. It doesn't matter at all that the green glass vase has a big chip out of the thick lip that protrudes 'artistically' on one side. As Stevie places it on his bedside locker the priest smiles gently. "Thank you."

"My pleasure," calls Arthur. "Our pleasure. You know, I've enjoyed our talks. Perhaps when we're out of here you would come and have a meal with us. Stevie cooks an excellent boeuf Bourguignonne."

The good feeling behind Arthur's invitation: Stevie rests in it absolutely, it's walled off from any scavenging doubt like some people's belief in God. Stevie is reminded just how good-looking Arthur still is, in a Gordon Brownish way.

"I should like that very much," says the priest. His voice, which seems composed of a sort of delicate outward wheeze, presumably in consequence of whatever disease laid him in this hospital bed, nevertheless contains nothing but untainted gratitude, untainted kindness. While Arthur continues, with eloquent inflections, "Or should you be vegetarian, then I have *every* confidence my Stevie could manage boeuf Bourguignonne without boeuf," Stevie is exultant with a question, just one: whether they will get to know the priest well enough to ask him where did he ever find an adult size in teddy-bear pyjamas.

THE PLACE OF RELIGION
IN MODERN THOUGHT

"The eyes—they're all you can see of it."

Because of the frenzied barking that crashes upon them from cages and coops all along the open shed, Jamie has to lean close to Alex to make himself heard, though he's careful not to lean too close. In darkness behind a grille, white orbs flash rhythmically, openings for disorder threatening the whole world.

Jamie continues, "Look how it's leaping up-down, up-down, like clockwork. That dog has been driven *mad.*"

"So you've become an expert on mental illness in dogs since you've been on your own." Anxiety caused Jamie to hear Alex easily above the barrage. Beneath the barking there are thumps and bangs as dogs hurl themselves against walls or wire. They're penned singly or in pairs.

Jamie wants to say, "Been on my own, have I?" but in fact says, "I don't think we speak of mental *illness* these days. We are supposed to say mental health *problems.*"

Sod it, he's fallen back into the sort of teasing challenge that marked so many of their old conversations. But it's comforting, like giving yourself a meal you remember from childhood, a boiled egg with fingers of buttered bread.

The dogs' noise is still going on even now that the track has brought Alex and Jamie to the benevolent double-dormered farmhouse, stone-built, honeyed in the morning sunshine, *1790* carved in the door lintel. There's no-one about, which relieves Jamie of the business of asking permission to go through the farm to get onto the hill. He needs the energy for a very different confrontation that's been brewing ever since his ex-, if a man of 48 can talk of having an ex-, 'phoned out of the blue to suggest going for a hike.

But for the moment Jamie just adds, "No, not *problems*. Mental health *issues*. Everything these days is an *issue*. Doctors don't deal with health *matters*, they deal with health *issues*. Why do we speak as if everything is a matter of dispute?"

Yes, the cue still works. Alex embarks on one of his lectures on the social and political implications of language. "Once there was a presumption that everyone had essentially the same feelings, so we have words like 'charming', which means that it's likely to charm *everyone*. But now we have the opposite presumption, that people vary enormously in their sentiments and tastes, so we assume that everything is a matter of dispute, an *issue*." But then he laughs in a way that he never did after his homilies of old. He turns to look at the view, walking backwards.

Below them is a panorama of peace and blessing: newly-green fields, ewes and lambs in profusion, the sun in a high blue sky expanding the heart with a message of the kindness of nature.

"It's so All-in-the-April-Evening. I thooooouuuuuuuught of the Laaaaamb of Gaaaawwwwwddd." Jamie parodies the mincing diction of a pious singer of the song. The renewal of the earth in spring has to be an omen that Alex's love, too, is being renewed. Jamie says, "It's bloody cruel, those dogs cooped up."

"Oh, they'll get let out in due course. Plenty of sheep to work on." Alex still has his irritating omniscience, but the *Guardian*-reading concerned-citizen Alex that Jamie lived with for nineteen years wouldn't have been so dismissive of cruelty.

"But you were the good works one, taking stands. Dragging me to work in the women's refuge shop. Sending me out with your Iraq War leaflets. Don't dogs matter?" They're now well above the domestic huddle of the farmhouse and its outbuildings. "I'd love a dog. The love. The love people want from God, a dog's love. The devotion." He doesn't quite manage, "A dog doesn't leave you." He springs in a very carefree manner over a gate, and fields are left behind for open hillside.

"Without my fastidiousness about dog hairs everywhere, you could have got yourself one." *Could have got yourself,* not *Can get yourself:* does that carry a stronger implication that Alex means their separation is over?

"Out at work all day, how can I leave a dog by itself?" And Jamie's missed his footing and toppled full-length into the heather, releasing a warm cloud of sweetness that embraces them both. His "Fuck!", while natural enough at the tumble, is really about the fact that he's given away the state of his love-life, if someone of 48 can use that phrase; given away his domestic arrangements, anyway. He springs up immediately so that Alex won't think he's lying there waiting for Alex's arms to help him up. He says, "A dog doesn't leave you."

But it's too nice a day for ill humour. Sunshine kindles faith that it will end in joy greater than which none can be imagined. After all, what goes around comes around, you get what you deserve in life, and Jamie did nothing to deserve being dumped. They walk on in comfortable talk about safe topics like idiocies at their workplaces and Alex's nieces and nephews, all of whom Jamie mentions by name like someone displaying qualifications.

Then they're too hot for talk and it's too steep. They've gone separate ways to skirt peat hags. Alex, nimble and fast despite his stocky build, is some way off, ascending by a different shoulder from the one Jamie is puffing up. But they'll reunite at the summit—it's a symbol, Jamie is being shown something! For a moment Jamie sinks into the comfort of that thought, then says "For fuck's sake!" out loud to a bee nuzzling the heather.

At the breezy summit there's a big grin to welcome them. Someone has stuck a thick fence-post into the cairn and carved a face in it, crude yet skilful. They sit against the cairn and eat the sandwiches each made for himself, Jamie having feared it would be tempting fate to offer to make sandwiches for them both. The universe would have punished such presumption by causing Alex, at the end of the day, to say only, "Well, we must stay in touch."

After a while Jamie wriggles flat and now he's lulled beneath the breeze and the high rhapsody of larks in an invisible layer of pure warmth and pure peace. The earth breathes goodness; its scents evoke salad and cricket bats. The face in the fence-post, upside-down to Jamie, smiles a blessing on him, and on Alex, and, yes, on the pair of them.

"Christ, listen!" Jamie sits up. "Can't you hear them? Up here, even. The dogs. Miles away. You can't even see the farm."

"Have you forgotten I'm a little hard of hearing?" He still doesn't trim his ear hair.

"I can hear them, I tell you. Still locked up. Someone should do something. Report the farmer."

"Jamie, it's nothing to do with you. Not your responsibility. Vengeance is mine, saith the Lord. Just enjoy the day, Jamie."

As though a snake had slithered out through the rocks of the cairn, Jamie is on his feet on behalf of the old secular Alex. "What's this religious crap? Christ, you've not turned to religion for comfort?"

He's pleased to have suggested that Alex might be the one in need of comfort even though it was he who initiated the break-up, but this satisfaction melts away before the implication in Alex's last words that they are just enjoying a day together, no more.

"It was only a phrase. I only meant that you can't take on everything. Perhaps I pushed too hard to drag you into my concerns, onto committees and things. You getting mugged stuffing those Iraq leaflets through doors in Possilpark." He's gathering up both lots of sandwich wrappings.

"So you have that much influence over me, getting me doing things against my will."

"Jamie, you've suffered enough, you can't take on all the world's suffering."

"Jesus did. I can do Biblical allusions, too. Anyway, I'm not taking on all the world's suffering. Just the dogs' suffering." And then, to have a pee, he pointedly turns away from the man he slept naked with for two decades, saying as he pees, "If you had responsibilities only because God handed them out, like an office manager giving out tasks, a celestial e-mail to my desk every day telling me exactly what I've to do...well, then, if I'm not sent the e-mail *Stop the dogs' suffering*, okay, then it's not my responsibility. Not in my job description. But God doesn't exist, so responsibilities aren't limited. It *is* my responsibility. Yours too. Child abuse next door—is that not my business, either? For fuck's sake, just accept that I do distress at cruelty to dogs, you have your standing orders to the Red Cross Disaster Fund and Amnesty." His anger can't jeopardise getting back together, because what's for you won't go by you. A heat haze dims the higher peaks of Ben Vorlich and Stuc a' Chroin. They're not just more hills: you have to be unimaginably different to be up there.

"I've had to cut back on the standing orders since it's been just my salary, Jamie."

What does that mean? Still turned away peeing, Jamie can't see Alex's face. Is he supposed to reply, "Well, it needn't be just *your* salary"? Would they be getting back together, not because Alex still loves you after all and can't believe the awful mistake he made, but because it would facilitate his charitable giving?

And Alex addressing him as "Jamie" even when there's no-one else around he needs distinguishing from.... This habit, thoroughly analysed, discloses a hundred reasons why their relationship was never meant to be. The flood of gratitude Jamie feels for this revelation sends him striding ahead in the descent. A lanky gawky moody teenager of forty-eight stumping off to his room after a family row? So what?

And then he halts: there's movement lower down. A quad bike approaches effortlessly, almost bouncing uphill. This must be the farmer, a laconic and suspicious countryman, zooming up to reprimand them for trespassing even though everyone says there's no law of trespass in Scotland. The quad bike stops a few yards away, releasing silence.

"Nice day," says the man. Jamie sifts the remark for menace. The long sideburns on the thin age-indeterminate face confirm the man's cruelty to dogs.

"Isn't it?" Alex, cheerily.

The man surveys the view. He's slight like a jockey: could he pull sheep and tractors out of ditches? His denims are too clean. Jamie, who knows about cheap after-shaves, is amazed by a whiff of *Lynx*.

"Have you, like, lost some sheep?" Jamie manages, opening a route to talking about sheepdogs and thence to their suffering. He feels the *Shut up* nudge Alex will give him when he does mention it.

"Not so far as I know," says the man. It's a well-known technique of intimidation, to postpone what you really have to say. "Sometimes I just have to get up here. You'll know what I mean. On the hills you can't help feeling grateful you're alive."

"Grateful to whom or what, exactly?" If Jamie can mount the secularist's challenge on that, why can't he challenge the man about the dogs?

"We liked the carved fence-post at the top." Alex, affably.

"And up here I'm away from the wife, too." The man's over-long laugh plainly invites them to join in a jokey moan about demanding wives, and this is plainly oppressive of gays, but protesting about that would be a diversion from going on the attack about the dogs, and then a gobsmack doubles Jamie's confusion when Alex says, "Well, we're a gay couple but we have our version of the sentiment."

Jamie is laughing with astonishment, nothing else. "No we're not!"

The man nods. "You're meant for each other, meant to be."

But already he's started the quad bike and without so much as a goodbye is skimming up the hill again. His last words could be just sarcastic or contemptuous, yet they resound with a guarantee, recalling tales in which words have mysterious authority because the speaker may seem ordinary, a beggar or a boatman, but is really some legendary supernatural being in disguise, like the Wandering Jew or Jesus or a fey prophesying creature from Gaelic mythology.

Jamie calls after the farmer, "*Meant* for each other? No-one is meant for anyone, because there's no divine wedding planner, no celestial Hello Dolly Levi planning who's to get together with whom." Now he's ready for Alex and snaps, "What did you say that for? I mean, you were always so don't-ask-don't-tell-none-of-their-business."

"Yes, but you always wanted to be more in-your-face about it."

"Yes, but to lie."

Will Alex say, "Well, we could make it true"? But now words must be set aside because here are steep outcrops of rock and you're concentrating on your footing, sometimes gripping the coarse straggly branches of the securely-rooted heather. The conversational bleatings of the sheep below and the fields that are an image of peace and blessing produce a homecoming feeling, but once they reach the track leading off the open hillside, the feeling is destroyed by the massed demonic barking from the dog-shed that's reaching new heights of intensity and rage. Mere howling would have produced softer feelings, mere melancholy; this is chaos declaring war.

"Still jumping up-down, up-down in that mad robotic way," Jamie shouts as he scurries past the open shed. Safely beyond, he adds, "I'd be as bad as the farmer himself if I stood by and did nothing about it."

"That's silly, Jamie. These dogs would still have been suffering even if you'd not been here at all. You're not to blame. Your presence or absence makes no difference."

Alex walks on so slowly that he might have been trying deliberately to avoid an air of having delivered a decisive retort.

And that's when Jamie's eye is caught by the single strand of barbed wire strung above the charming dry-stane dyke that borders the track; caught by a series of black blobs with tiny appendages, each blob hand-stuck on its barb a meticulous four barbs from the next. Beyond the wall a gang of exploring lambs charges about among munching ewes. The blobs are moles, shovel hands and delicate snouts exposed. Jamie begins to count them: an even number and there'll be reunion by nightfall. A blob moves. That has to be the sweet warm gentle spring breeze, no-one could have impaled a live mole.

Suddenly the benign grin in the fence-post dissolves, is gone entirely. There's only dead wood with hacked indentations, the lovely landscape of peace and blessing is a flimsy delusive film projected upon unyielding rock, and the suffering of dogs is nothing but a motion of atoms. Not only is there no-one to hand out duties like an office manager distributing tasks, but the world is not, after all, a limitless domain for the free exercise of conscience, for it's suddenly clear that nothing *matters*.

Jamie hurries to catch Alex up. "You're right, it's not my business." It will strike him in the middle of the night, in the midst of happiness, that he left the live twisting mole stuck on its barb, and will reproach himself for fleeing into forgetfulness from the task of horrible mercy-killing.

When Alex drops him at his flat, Jamie asks, "Do you

want to come in?" It's as awkward as an invitation 'for coffee' after a disco decades before.

"I can see where you've been living," says Alex. More hopeful than *I can see where you live.*

There's mail. Jamie stoops to lift it, Alex shuts the front door behind them as though it were his business to do so.

Leaflet…'phone bill…postcard from someone Jamie saw a few times last autumn…another leaflet, about home-delivered pizza.

He turns back to the first leaflet.

"Christ!"

There has to be a reason why this leaflet is here just at this moment. It's from an animal welfare charity. The front shows a starving mongrel with sticking-out ribs and a hurt mournful face that yearns to love you in spite of all the bad you've done. The dog was left in a locked flat when its owner went to America. It pawed a cupboard door ajar and tried to bite open unyielding tins.

"A sign, a message," Jamie says it ironically, of course. Equally ironically he adds, "Being sent a message makes you feel sort of noticed. Cherished, even, which I haven't felt much lately."

"So you got the message! I tried to get it across to you every ten minutes on that bloody hill and thought I'd failed. It's what the man said, Jamie, we are meant to be together. You can't love someone without believing that." He kisses Jamie.

"No, no," Jamie says when he can speak again, meaning that Alex misunderstood what message he was referring to, the universe nudging you with a leaflet, an imaginary message, for there aren't any signs or message like that. But Alex will misunderstand that *No, No,* and Jamie quickly covers with, "You *can* love someone without believing it's meant to be. I do." It strikes him that the animal welfare people waited to photograph the dog before feeding it.

They say all that is necessary for reunion, then Jamie waves the pizza leaflet and says, "We've had a sign what the celebration meal's to be. Let's send out for a pizza. Oh, I forgot, you don't eat junk food."

"I may not have done in the past."

Jamie picks up the phone and dials, feeling like a character in a book whose author always planned that his time of trial was to have a happy ending. "I want to report cruelty to dogs. It's on a farm near Stirling." He eyes Alex defiantly.

THE PARTY FROM ENGLAND

"Bill used to say, in the open air you can always find somebody to have sex with."

Donald concentrates on finding firm footholds across a squelchy stretch. He rises on tip-toes to keep his trousers above the dirt, real trousers in contrast to the jeans all the others are wearing except the one who's just spoken, the one with a shaved head and big walrus moustache, who's in black leather trousers. Donald's dark suit and overcoat are, of course, totally unsuitable for traipsing up a mountain, but it's a matter of *respect*.

Of which they are showing precious little.

"But I bet he fucking never scored here," the voice continues, a hollow one fit to express menace; though the answering burst of laughter makes Donald think, just for a moment, of a schoolmistress articulating the children's responses to nature for them.

"Maybe he did it with a sheep. Humping away while it lies there and thinks of England."

"Scotland, dear. We're in a foreign country."

After a pause during which you can hear their breaths labouring with the ascent: "There might have been some hairy Scotsman lurking behind a rock." That one's tall and bespectacled and skinny, so skinny one wonders about his state of health, though he seems to have energy enough, leaping off rocks, landing with skateboarder poses. He's got pale straight hair and a weak slack mouth, and whenever he speaks he looks anxiously round at the rest for a response.

Don't quarrel with them, Donald instructs himself again. Even though, as it happens, he is very hairy. He, at least, can respect the solemnity of the occasion. The immense landscape is mournful even beyond what the occasion requires, mountain summits shrouded in fast-moving cloud, last year's grass withered beyond hope of renewal, obliterating rain sweeping in again and again. He turns to walrus-moustache: "Where are—?"

Walrus-moustache's face gathers into the polite mask a hotel manager presents to a guest. "Steve has them. Bill's partner."

Donald's own love for Kirsty rises up like insulation.

"Oh, right. I didn't catch all the names when you arrived."

Walrus-moustache nods ahead at a young man struggling to maintain his balance while heaving upwards a large green polythene canister. Something to lug petrol or water about in. At least he's wearing a sensible fleecy jacket. One or two of them are in shirt sleeves—don't these people feel the cold? The young man pauses to get his breath, smiles back at walrus-moustache. Donald notes sparkling eager eyes, a smile unaffected by cynicism or constraint, hair traditionally neat-and-tidy. A lot younger than William. *Partner.*

"That thing. That's—?"

"The ashes."

So they hadn't bothered with a proper urn, something polished and solemn. But then, he had been left out of it all, and apparently it was all perfectly legal: a will, ashes to be scattered at the Rest and Be Thankful Pass, this Steve executor instead of himself.

And he'd had to wait nearly two hours at the car park before the party from England arrived after their overnight drive. It had soon become clear that something must be done. As they disembarked from the minibus someone had produced a camera, Donald had been hauled into a line of them, the others had kicked up their legs for the picture, he'd been forced to do the same. Disengaging, he was inspired to say, "Now, as for the actual place for the scattering, there's a special place that William had private memories of up that hill there, Beinn an Lochain. A place where it levels into a green arena, a sort of balcony looking down over the pass and Glen Croe. Quite a way up."

"Mountaineering? These denims are Armani."

"Who's this Ben-someone?"

"Dunno, but his middle name is *Anne*. Got his number!"

For a time it had seemed likely he'd succeeded, that some of them, at least, would opt to stay behind at the minibus, but then walrus-moustache had said, "We'll do what Donald suggests," and that was that.

Now, as they all trudge upwards, Donald's memory of that special place wavers: perhaps it was on a different hill. Certainly there's no sign of a green balcony in the gloomy twisted hillside. The trace of a path is getting steeper, and as Donald strains his leg up to a rock ledge a hand is stretched out to him from above. At the car-park this tubby one had been holding a cigarette like someone at a cocktail party, hand arched back, elbow tight in. The face, in which there's something cherubic gone bad, simpers as he holds out his hand, but his eyes are slits of cold calculation.

"All right?" The question resonates beyond the subject of Donald's footing.

"Yes, thank you. I'm used to the hills."

"Yes, you being Scottish." He makes it sound enviable,

like being royalty.

One smooth-soled black shoe slithers, the other knee bangs forward onto rock, Donald has to take cocktail-smoker's hand after all.

"Thank you." Donald has pulled himself up, tries to free his hand. Dirt on trouser knee, on overcoat.

"No problem. So where do you live?" Cocktail-smoker, turning to face the line of ascent again, has actually transferred Donald's hand to his other hand, holding it so tightly it would be rude to use the degree of force necessary to free it.

"Helensburgh."

"I've never been to Helens-*bruh*." They are hand-in-hand like schoolchildren in a crocodile, cocktail-smoker stumbling through heather and boulders because the path isn't wide enough for two.

Cocktail-smoker murmurs, "You know, I don't have to go back with the others."

Then: "I can stay just as long as you want."

Donald has snatched back his hand as if he'd touched an electrified fence. "I'm engaged to be married."

He tells cocktail-smoker, "In six weeks' time."

"That's all right, mate. I don't mind being the condemned man's last meal."

But here's walrus-moustache conveniently at Donald's elbow, asking, "Is it much further, this place?"

"Well…in case the rain comes on again perhaps I should do it here." There's the inane burst of laughter that would inevitably accompany the last few words on what pass for comedy shows on television these days.

Walrus-moustache restores order: "Okay, guys, Donald says this is where."

The hillside here is steep enough to give a drop for the

scattering and the view is splendid, or would be if the trough of Glen Croe between its mountain walls, deep below the snaking road that is itself distant below them, weren't dimmed by drifting patches of rain and mist. Donald positions himself above the others on a wee outcrop of rock, reaches out to take the canister from this Steve.

"I can manage, Donald, thanks." His heartbreaking smile as he comes forward—what would be a heartbreaking smile in any other person—makes Donald step back from his chosen position in spite of himself.

Steve has actually occupied the outcrop, is fiddling with the canister cap. Where's walrus-moustache?

"Steve's doing the scattering, Donald."

"But I'm his brother."

But the others have lowered their heads, and Donald automatically does the same.

"We've all got our own special memories of Bill," says walrus-moustache. "Donald, of course. Steve most of all. You two were so right together. I know I speak for everyone here when I say this, and, really, there's nothing else worth saying: you were one hell of a guy, Bill. Okay, Steve, let her rip!"

Donald says long-sufferingly, "Amen."

Steve swings the canister backwards and forwards a few times like a discus-thrower limbering up, getting the measure of the task, and then, with nothing but energy in his face, he hurls. Something greyish-white gushes forth, Steve has swung again, hurled again, more spurts out. And then there is a great bellow of wind, the wind sweeps up the steepness before them, the ash streaming from Steve's canister is whirled up into huge clouds that blow back over them, on them, all amid the desolation of rock, depth, far-off forests. They shout and gasp, voices lost and blown away.

"You fucker, Bill McLachlan, you absolute fucker."

"I'm breathing you in, I'm *swallowing* you."

"Nothing new for you." The skinny one, a bit after the others. Rightly ignored.

Steve is oblivious, he's in a rhythm, a fervent rhythm, his body swings back and forth. The buttocks in his jeans look perfectly ordinary for someone who'd been in that sort of relationship.

"There's so much ash. I always you thought you burnt down to, like, a handful."

"Well, he was so-o-o-o *big*. In *every* way." Growled in a parody of a voluptuous voice.

At last the ash gives out, Steve staggers backwards from the sudden weightlessness of the canister. The wind drops to nothing.

No, there isn't silence.

"Hey, listen."

It's a new-born plea on that vast bleak stony mountainside. It's the most timid tentative bleat imaginable.

They look in all directions, peer around rises, into dips.

"Hey, it's a lamb." The skinny one.

He's staring down into a gully where a burn trickles among dirty crusts of old snow and last year's rusty dead bracken. There it is, the tiniest little thing, so pure and white, wobbly on its pipe-cleaner legs. Now it's bleating as though it can't stop, with perfect rhythm, perfect pathos, a toy lamb in which the sound mechanism has stuck.

The skinny one says, "Hello, little chap," crouches, holds out an inviting hand.

"Hey, maybe Bill did shag a sheep and this one is his

son turning up to see dad off."

"Don't touch it!" Donald, fiercely.

Donald rebukes: "If it gets a man's hands over it, its mother will smell the human scent and reject it."

"So-o-o-o true. My mother rejected *me* when a man put his hands all over me."

The lamb has tottered towards the skinny one, and now its mouth settles on a finger-tip.

"Hey, it thinks my little finger is its mother's nipple."

"It thinks your little finger is your dick. It's heard about Simon's *small* problem."

The skinny one gives a gratified smile, glasses obscured by raindrops. His crouching pose shows up just how thin he is. That disease: not what William died of, thank God.

"We'd better try to find its mother." Walrus-moustache.

"Its mother could be dead."

"Maybe a wolf ate her."

"We *do not* have wolves in Scotland."

Donald realises he only has walrus-moustache's word that William died of a heart attack. Having been excluded from registering his brother's death. And from everything else. To be fair, walrus-moustache had been in touch about things, 'phoning him up quite a lot, and it wasn't their fault he hadn't been at the funeral. Nevertheless...

"We'd better spread out and call," says walrus-moustache, and someone calls, "Hey, you! Hey, *ewe!*—e-w-e." Laughter.

"No, call like the lamb. Bleat."

"Baa!" It's baritonal.

"Not like that. Lighter and higher." Walrus-moustache's growling bass issues a perfect replica of the lamb's bleat and they all look to see whether it recognises a brother's cry, but it's back to emitting its mechanical evenly-spaced bleats, oblivious of their concern for it.

"Come on!"

"Oh, he's so-o-o-o masterful in his leather trousers."

They all spread out across the mountainside, Donald too, each choosing a little prominence, finding a secure footing. Drifts of drizzle or cloud blur the more distant of them. They're nine sentinels or guardian saints, nine Gaelic warriors from Ossian's poems of heroism and slaughter, nine useless fenceposts with the connecting wire long gone, as you sometimes find on hills. Cocktail-smoker's tubby outline holds a cigarette in its cocktail-party pose, elbow in, hand arched back.

Walrus-moustache brings them in like a conductor. "One-two-three. Me-e-eh."

"Me-e-eh."

"Me-e-eh."

There is just the sound of wind, a seeping of water everywhere. Even their lamb is silent.

"Again."

"Me-e-eh."

"Me-e-eh."

"Me-e-eh."

It strikes Donald that leather trousers, so unsuitable anyway, will shrink in the rain: in some boyhood cowboy story wasn't someone tied up in rawhide that would shrink when wet, as a torture?

"Me-e-eh."

"Me-e-eh."

Cocktail-smoker ambles back towards walrus-moustache like someone who's got all the entertainment he can out of this. "We're frightening its mother off, keeping her away. The sooner we get out of here the better." He throws down his cigarette stub; Donald glares.

"Better for the lamb," cocktail-smoker adds propitiatingly. But his eyes remain calculating slits.

The others are straggling back, too.

"We may find a farm and can report it."

"They look cuddly and helpless but they're survivors."

"I'm cuddly and helpless, too." The skinny one. It doesn't get a response.

Is it true that if you touch a lamb its mother will reject it? It strikes Donald that farmers handle lambs all the time. Perhaps it's young deer, fawns, that that's supposed to apply to.

Only Steve is still at his post, the empty green canister wedged between his denimed legs, his hands cupped. "Me-e-eh. Me-e-eh."

"We're going back, Steve." Walrus-moustache.

Steve's smile as he rejoins them is so much like one of goodness and distress. What's he doing among this crowd? "I just don't like to leave it," he says as they set off downhill.

"Drinks at the Arrochar Hotel."

"Is it gay?"

"It will be when we get there."

"They won't know what's hit them."

"Look, we do know about such things in Scotland."

"Look," Donald adds protestingly, "William and I used to have afternoon tea in the Arrochar Hotel when we were boys."

They're hurrying now, the rain is getting worse.

He says, "On a Sunday afternoon Dad would drive us all out for a trip and we'd often end up there for tea."

No-one seems to understand.

Donald says, "Once when we went there, it was after

we'd been up Beinn an Lochain. I could only have been about eight, I couldn't make it to the top. William said he'd wait with me while Dad and Mum went on to the top. In that green balcony."

He makes it clear to them: "That's the sort of person he was *really* like."

"That's great." Steve. "I wish I'd known him as long as you. Then again, I don't. The loss would be so much worse."

"It is."

Steve has halted, Donald involuntarily halts with him, and Steve is saying, "I thought I could still hear the lamb there but maybe I'm just imagining it."

"Nevertheless," Donald says in the magnanimous way in which he would decline to press charges against a homeless down-and-out for trying to snatch money at a cash machine, "since you were, well, close to my brother, my condolences."

"That's okay."

It sounds a bit too much like someone accepting an apology.

Donald makes up his mind he will not go to the Arrochar Hotel with this crew. He will just say he'd rather not because of his memories. Which would be true. And no-one could think him rude, his grief as brother entitles him not to go. But as they slither and stumble against each other, discovering it's always harder going down than up, he fears he will be too weak not to.

THE USES OF LITERATURE

The story, nicely word-processed, arrives in the post three days before Laura is due to come to dinner. A note on paper printed all over with very pale flowers says, "I'd love to have your reactions to this story. We could discuss it over dinner, if I'm still invited."

"What do you mean, *if I'm still invited*?" Michael says down the 'phone. "Why would we do that? Disinvite you?"

"I'm really glad."

That's so heartfelt that Michael's writer's brain, accustomed to inventing plausible conversational exchanges, twitches at something odd.

No, it's just that Laura is so very earnest about making people feel good about themselves that she overplays it.

He warns her, "But remember, just because I've had a few things published, that doesn't mean I'm any help on someone else's writing."

Somehow, that doesn't seem to be what she wants to hear. He placates her with special intimacy. "Harry's doing the cooking, so it'll be something for you and me to talk about while he's in the kitchen."

"Oh. But it's for him to read, too."

"Okay. But Harry's not the bookish type."

"I don't think I'm clever enough to write for bookish people, Michael. I write what I *feel*."

That's so Laura, Michael reflects when they ring off: determined to be unsophisticated but confident she's still a match for the ways of the world. *Steely naïveté*, you could call it; maybe symbolised by the dresses she wears, thin, drab, drooping, much-washed, somehow more suited to little girls than to someone as tall and borderline skinny as she is, but perhaps worn to make a deliberate statement that, as an independent, un-needy woman, she's no need of the artifices of fashion and make-up...

"So I'm not the bookish type. Just your hairy rugby-playing bit of rough." Harry interrupts Michael's musings.

"No, sorry, you do read books."

"Almost human, isn't he?"

"No, sorry, I just meant, well, not, like, nerdy and geeky about books and writing like me."

Harry makes the noise *Hmm*.

"She wants you to read it," Michael says, as if offering a further apology.

"Okay," Harry says, as if accepting it.

*   *   *

Martin is the name of Laura's story. Michael always thinks calling a story by the name of a character is a cop-out but of course there's distinguished precedent: *Emma*, *Clarissa*, *Anna Karenina*, lots of Dickens...

The protagonist of *Martin* is Liz, who'd known this Martin at college. "I had a bit of a crush on him. To be honest, a big crush." We aren't told about anything that happened, not even whether they ever went on a date, but there's lots about her feelings.

> At the sexual level, Martin was
> very sexually attractive. But it
> wasn't only that I knew he could
> satisfy me sexually.

Michael can just hear Laura saying that, her small voice resolute about being frank, at least in the sanitising language she's become fluent in from the personal growth workshops and Gestalt groups and mindfulness sessions she frequents.

> My feelings were more extensive and meaningful on many different levels. I guess I was focusing on him the cocktail of needs and emotions that people call love. Although I knew real relationships involve negotiating compromises between different people's needs, I felt I was having the experience of finding "the one." Using visualisation, I felt close to him as lover, friend, companion, father of my children, as guiding and protecting me, and as a child himself.

And so on.

But apparently he'd shown no romantic interest in her, and when they left college they'd gone their separate ways.

Years later, Liz moves to Edinburgh. She learns from her mother, "who I've had to work through a lot of issues with", that Martin now lives there, too. Her mother knows this because she used to play doubles tennis with Martin's mother "at national level" and they have stayed friends, though it is emphasised (why?) that they don't know Liz and Martin are already acquainted. We are given a long telephone chat between the mothers in which they discover and comment on the coincidence of their offspring living in the same city, and Martin's mother gives his 'phone number to Liz's mother, urging her to pass it on to Liz in case she needs help settling in Edinburgh.

It felt like we were meant to meet up again. I was understandably nervous about phoning him but took my courage in both hands. We arranged to meet for a meal. I walked in with butterflies in my tummy, wondering if the old feelings would still be there, but as soon as I saw him I knew at once they were dead.

Over delicious Chinese food he told me he identified as gay and I understood why I no longer had feelings for him. In her book *Sex and Relationships in Modern Society*, Nancy Reinhold says that sexual attraction in modern society has lost its connection with reproduction and is all about seeking and receiving validation. You are attracted to the people you think will validate you in return by being attracted to you, and our selfish genes mean that we don't waste emotional energy in being attracted to people who cannot return our feelings, so logically I would not have feelings for Martin any more.

Later, Hugh, Martin's partner, arrived to give him a lift home. In his slate-grey eyes I saw real caringness, and was truly glad Martin had someone who cared for him. Hugh insisted on offering me one, too. He dropped Martin off first, because Martin had things he needed to do. Outside my flat Hugh and I sat talking in the car. I couldn't resist asking him about Martin. I guess I felt it was the nearest I was ever going to get to Martin. Then I realised that the caringness I saw in Hugh's eyes didn't have to be about only Martin. Suddenly I knew that Hugh was someone who I could entrust my life to, without any hesitation, knowing he would not injure or damage me in any way. I realised I had feelings for Hugh.

And there *Martin* ends.

Michael makes the noise *Hmm* to no-one in particular. Conscientiously, he tries to bat away the critical comments that flock to mind: perhaps he's just trying to reshape her story into something *he* would write, which wouldn't be respecting her creativity, or perhaps he just takes a nasty pleasure in fault-finding. But saying nothing isn't an option, because when Laura suggested they *could* discuss it over dinner, that meant she'd be politely ruthless in ensuring they *would* discuss it.

* * *

Over Harry's almond soup, which she pronounces in a very affirming way to be delicious, she says she wants to say how much she appreciated Michael's help when she started work at the public library, how much she has come to value their friendship, and how much she hopes nothing will damage it.

"Why should it?" Harry's bull neck and heavy face—heavy with bone rather than surplus flesh—can make him seem stern when he isn't. Laura, though, seems delighted that he said it.

During Harry's casserole of beans and seeds, for Laura is a vegetarian, she talks about the evening classes she's attending, one on creative writing and one on counselling. "They go together really, really well. Creative writing helps you discover your true feelings and work through them."

"That's amazing!" Harry's voice and stunned look say he's been given a world-transforming insight. Usually he's very tolerant of Laura. Could sarcasm to someone who's more Michael's friend mean he's still smarting from the *not bookish* comment? Luckily she tends not to perceive irony.

"I know," she's saying eagerly. "When I start my counselling practice, creative writing is going to be a really important part of it. What you make your characters do discloses an awful lot about your motivations and who you really are. So does reacting to other people's creative writing."

When Harry, hands in red-striped oven gloves, is bringing in the pear clafoutis, Laura says "Yummy!" before she can see what it is. Then she says, "So how does my story make you feel? It's a really good sign that you still wanted me to be here after reading it."

Michael says, "Why wouldn't we?" and Harry, placing the dish on a heat-resistant table-mat, says, "I'm sure Michael has lots of bookish comments on structure, style, etcetera."

Laura says, "I meant about the new situation."

Michael says, "What situation?"

"The fact that I have feelings for Harry and how we are going to deal with this."

"*What?*"

She says gently, "I don't think you can really be surprised, Michael, after reading my story."

"But—but—it was a *story*!"

"I wrote it to break the new situation to you."

"I thought you wanted comments on it as, like, literature."

"Bookish comments," Harry glosses.

"It might be worth," says Laura, like someone trying to persuade a child to give up a stolen white mouse they've stuffed in a pocket, "asking yourself why you didn't see the message it was conveying. You could have been hiding some awareness from yourself."

Harry murmurs, "He didn't even get the reference to my grey eyes." He's smiling at Laura—smiling encouragement?

Michael gets up, walks to the sideboard, returns to his chair, sits down again.

"But—but—it's absurd. I mean, we're a *gay* couple. These feelings you have for Harry, he's not going to return them, is he?"

Suddenly the metaphor of the ground falling away from under your feet strikes home as the best metaphor ever. "Are you, Harry?"

Harry's still serving the clafoutis.

Laura's voice is still gentle. "Don't you think it's not a good idea to put labels on ourselves, instead of getting in touch with who we really are, behind the labels?"

"But a gay man is what Harry really is. The label's true. He fancies blokes, not women."

He reins back from saying, "His cock doesn't get hard for women, so hard cheese."

He says it.

Laura's voice, always respectful and understanding, adds forgiveness for the petulance that produced a bad word. "Harry's feelings could surprise you."

"You mean you two have actually," Michael says, "talked about this?"

He stares accusation at Harry but still can't catch his eye.

Michael says, "Slept together?"

"Not yet, Michael," Laura says. "But I must have sensed in him the potential for returning my feelings or I wouldn't be having those feelings."

Explaining, Laura's voice is very patient. "Nancy Reinhold—this was in my story—says in her book *Sex and Relationships in Modern Society* that in modern society sexual attraction has lost the connection with reproduction and is all about seeking and receiving validation. You feel attracted to people so they will validate you in return by being attracted to you. Selfish genes prevent us from wasting emotional energy being attracted to people who can't return our feelings. So I wouldn't be investing feelings in Harry unless I knew instinctively he was capable of providing the validation I'm looking for."

"You're saying if you fancy someone it means they fancy you back." Michael manages a savage laugh. "So every nutcase stalker who says, 'Deep down, you really love me'—like that stalker in Ian McEwan's *Enduring Love*—is right. Otherwise he wouldn't be attracted to him. Or her." Michael rolls his eyes as dramatically as he can, inviting Harry to do the same, but Harry is giving the cream a final stir.

Laura's face shows only concern for Michael. She says, "Stalking is *inappropriate* behaviour. Promoting stalking could get this Ian McEwan struck off from being a counsellor. Stalkers don't talk things *through* in an atmosphere of respect and reach a resolution of the situation mutually acceptable to both parties. Which is what we all have to do here. Harry and I will be supporting you, Michael. You're distressed; it could help to write a story on the theme of distress. Use the word to brainstorm."

"Right," he says. "Politeness over. Laura, you think you can just walk in and whisk Harry away from me because you *have feelings* for him. You can't. We don't want—" He realises with pride that he's honest enough to realise he can no longer speak for Harry, and amends that *We*. "I don't want anything more to do with you. Fuck off for ever and take your fucking psychobabble with you."

She gives Harry a what-are-we-going-to-do-with-him? look. Harry mirrors it back. "This isn't a mature reaction, Michael. Doctor Ron Wahid says maturity is not putting your head in the sand but coming to terms with *reality*."

"Harry, why aren't you helping here? Please, just tell her you don't fancy women so fuck off, end of story."

"I'm afraid," says Harry, "it wouldn't be any use."

The hem of his napkin is coming unstitched. Michael loves that bit of indifferent normality.

"However," Harry says, as though it were a complete sentence. Laura's look gives an ally carte blanche to say whatever he sees fit.

"About your story," Harry says. "It's no good going about it like that."

Her face is willing to learn.

Harry says, "I don't know much about writing but you

can't live with our own Doris Lessing here without some of it rubbing off. Those descriptions of your feelings—you felt this and you felt that…. Have you heard of *Show not tell?* You should hear Doris here go on about it: writers shouldn't *say* what someone's feelings are but must, like, imply them by what the person says and does. Sounds dumb to me—what's wrong with describing someone's feelings if you've got the right words?—but you just write gush, a mixture of teenage-girl-diary and horrible counselling jargon."

She flinches but her voice is brave. "I guess I'm not so worried as you about style and things. I try to be *honest.*"

"Honesty doesn't give you a proper story. It's just a snippet someone'd tell a friend. *I used to have a crush on this bloke at college but it turns out he's gay. Quite fancy his boyfriend.*"

Michael snatches at delighted literary agreement with Harry. "I thought that. It's just an *anecdote.*" But he's also sifting Harry's remarks for signs that Laura has been barking up the wrong tree.

"But basically it's *the truth,*" she protests. "I just altered details."

Harry waves the oven gloves. "Doesn't matter. It's not a story. Dunno how you make it one. Maybe clues mislead her: Martin's mourning a dead partner, Chris, who turns out, boom-boom, to have been Christopher not Christine. But that'd just be a feeble twist. Oh, you can leave things up in the air—I like that sometimes—but even when you're leaving things up in the air the story still needs that sense of having got somewhere. What the Master here calls *the resolution.*"

"The situation doesn't have a resolution yet." Her mouth, whose unlipsticked lips always look chapped, has turned pouty.

"Also, I don't take to the idea of writing stories and things to send messages to people. It sort of misses the point of proper writing. So does writing to boost your self-esteem or *work through*"—sarcastic emphasis there—"your feelings or discover who you are; therapy. If that's why you're writing, it's like, I don't know, like someone having a baby because they think the hormonal changes and so on will give them a nice complexion. Really, writers just need to think of pleasing the reader."

Falteringly, she says, "I'm trying to push away the idea that you're trying to undermine me, personally and professionally." But it seems she does push it away, and her voice manages a helpful-contribution tone: "In critiquing something, the rule is, three positive things for every negative thing."

Harry says, "But there aren't any positive things to say about it."

Tall skinny Laura really does look like a little girl as, in her little-girl mauve dress, she runs from the dining-table. From the hall her voice lets loose some determined sobbing. She calls, "You've empowered me to see that the relationship with you wouldn't have worked." The front door slams.

Harry tucks into his dessert as though nothing has happened. Michael, subdued into the same silence, follows suit.

The relationship, she said, not *a* relationship.

When they have finished their own desserts, their spoons, as if nothing is damaged, alternate in the one that would have been Laura's.

In the kitchen, as Harry scrapes plates for the dishwasher, Michael impedes him by putting his arms around him from behind. He says, "You certainly knew how to see her off."

As Harry resumes scraping Michael adds, "I mean, you didn't really have anything going with her, did you?—feelings for her?"

"What do *you* think?" says Harry, as if even to ask such a question must be preposterous. Harry's words call upon knowledge and confidence and trust that Michael has built up over the years, but suddenly those things aren't there. Laura's wicked words have made them vanish and will continue to work their poison for ever…

Michael's writer's brain twitches to the rescue. There's a story in what has happened, and if he can only write it, the missing confidence and trust, etcetera, might be retrieved, like a computer document you thought was lost. And think of the revenge on Laura if he got the story published and sent it to her! She opens the virgin volume with the immaculate paper-and-print smell, begins reading, realises that this is about *her*.…

As Harry washes the good wineglasses and Michael dries, Michael's writer's brain pursues the narrative: "Liz's story arrived in the post a few days before she was due to have dinner with us. She'd attached a note in her delicate italic handwriting that read, 'I've written this story. We could discuss it over dinner, if the invitation still stands…'"

CPSIA information can be obtained at www.ICGtesting.com
Printed in the USA
LVOW10s2018200116

471540LV00008B/906/P